GHOST CAVE

GHOST CAVE

BARBARA STEINER

HARCOURT BRACE JOVANOVICH, PUBLISHERS
San Diego   New York   London

Requests for permission to make copies of any part of the work
should be mailed to: Permissions Department,
Harcourt Brace Jovanovich, Publishers,
Orlando, Florida 32887.

Library of Congress Cataloging-in-Publication Data
Steiner, Barbara A.
Ghost cave/by Barbara Steiner.
p. cm.
Summary: In pursuit of a reward for the discovery of an Indian
burial site, Marc and two friends get lost in a cave inhabited by a
ghost.
ISBN 0-15-230752-4
[1. Indians of North America—Antiquities—Fiction.
2. Caves—Fiction. 3. Ghosts—Fiction.] I. Title.
PZ7.S825Gh   1990
[Fic]—dc20   89-26763

Printed in the United States of America

First edition
A B C D E

CONTENTS

For my nephew Mark Daniel,
who took me into the cave,
which was the beginning of my addiction
to the underworld.

1

THE REWARD POSTER

For the second time in a week, Marc felt he had to escape from home. Maybe it was the rain, the rain that had kept him prisoner in the house. School had let out, promising freedom. Then a week of rain had followed. It didn't seem fair. But then nothing in his life seemed fair lately.

He grabbed his yellow slicker. It was too small, but at least it would keep off some of the water. Jamming an old straw hat onto his head, he rolled his bike into the driveway.

Bluedog looked at him with her funny amber eyes, wiggled and whined, smiling an eager "Let's go!" look. Marc leaned over and tried to hug her, but she was in no mood for hugging. She tugged loose, bouncing and barking, impatient.

Marc laughed. He didn't know what he'd do without Bluedog. She seemed to be the only family member he could count on these days.

"Yes, girl, you can come." One foot on the pedal, Marc swung his leg over and coasted down the drive. He didn't think his dad had heard him leave. Or if he had, he wouldn't care.

Pine Creek was one of those small towns built around a square. Instead of a courthouse or a railroad station in the center, it had a park dotted with huge pine trees and bordered with magnolias.

He cut across the park, threading his way between the two picnic tables. A park bench, usually occupied by Grandpa Howe and Ephron McCully playing checkers, was empty. Too wet for them, too. A row of magnolias dripped, beads of water trickling down their shiny leaves. The week's steady downpour had eased, but the world smelled waterlogged.

A small crowd had gathered around the town bulletin board. It announced band concerts in the park, summer classes at the recreation building, lost dogs and cats. Marc stopped to find out what was up.

"Hey, Schaller, you see this sign?" Howard Moon hollered at Marc before he got close.

Howard Moon, nicknamed Mooney, was a pain in the you-know-what. Surely he could see that Marc had just gotten there and hadn't read the sign. Marc ignored him and squeezed in between Grandpa and Ephron, to see what Mooney was so excited about.

REWARD:

Fifty dollars, cash money, for information leading to the discovery of any Indian graves in Franklin or Johnson County. I would prefer the graves be left undug, but I'll buy any relics newly found if I can see their location.

ANDY BESLOW
Collector/Dealer

Signed this tenth day of June, 1954.

Fifty dollars! Boy howdy, anyone would be excited about that amount of money. But Marc held down his desire to run right out and start looking. He pretended to be casual about the whole thing. He sure didn't want Mooney getting the idea that he knew where any relics were.

"Who's Andy Beslow?" he asked instead. Mr. Daniels was the only collector and dealer he knew around Pine Creek.

"Beslow's a professor down there at the university," Ephron McCully told Marc. "I figure he's gotta be desperate for some Indian relics. Why, I remember when you could pick 'em up in any farmer's field around here."

"Yep, there were plenty of flint spears and arrowheads over at the river, under the bluffs," Grandpa Howe added. Alex Howe wasn't Marc's grandfather. Everyone in town had called him that as long as Marc could remember. He was a good person to consult for Pine Creek history.

"You figure on taking up that Andy Beslow's offer, Schaller?" Mooney asked, acting real friendly.

Right away Marc was suspicious. Mooney was no friend of his. He was the biggest kid in fifth grade because he'd flunked third two years before. He didn't have any friends unless you counted Otis Kruger. Otis was what people in Pine Creek called "poor white trash." His father stayed drunk all the time, and nobody knew where his mother was. Sometimes Marc felt sorry for Otis. But he'd never wasted one minute feeling sorry for Mooney.

"I don't know," Marc said, acting casual again about the poster. "How 'bout you?"

Mooney could see that Marc hadn't bought into his friendly act. "Naw, too much work. But everyone in town knows you're the expert. Maybe I'll just let you find something for me, Schaller. You and your kiddie friends do the legwork, and I'll help you collect the reward."

Mooney grinned, showing the front tooth he'd broken on the jungle gym before school let out. Then he went to pick up his bike where he'd laid it on the curb. On the handlebars two canvas bags gaped, half full of newspapers. Was Mooney this late finishing his paper route? It was almost eight-thirty.

Maybe if Mooney lost his job for being late all the time, Marc could get it. If he could earn some money, he could buy some new relics from Mr. Daniels to add to his collection. Marc and his dad had the best Indian-relic collection in town except for Mr. Daniels—but then, he was a dealer. They spent all their spare time hunting and digging for new pieces. Or they had, until January.

Marc pushed the thought way down inside. He took pride in his ability to control his mind. Thinking about the past wasn't worth all the bad feelings it brought. He'd had enough bad feelings this spring to last him a lifetime.

He whistled to Bluedog, who was inspecting the park's garbage cans. They'd go see if Hermie was up.

Hermie lived behind the Pine Creek library and down two blocks. As Marc rode, he wondered about the poster. Was there any possibility of finding a grave that hadn't already been disturbed in Johnson or any other county? Boy howdy, that'd sure be a treasure worth hunting for, even without the reward.

He stood up on the pedals and pumped harder. The summer was looking somewhat better. Just wait till Hermie and Eddie heard about the possibility of earning fifty dollars for doing what they'd planned to do all summer anyway. Marc laughed out loud at the thought.

2

A PLAN

"Hi, Hermie." Marc entered the sleeping porch without knocking. Through the screens he could see his friend still in bed, not asleep, but reading.

Hermie pushed up his wire glasses from where they'd slipped down his nose. His pajamas were getting too small, and his belly showed around the middle. 'Course, Hermie's belly seemed to show underneath whatever he wore, since it was fairly round.

"Hey, Marc. Did you know there were three Civil War battles fought in this part of Arkansas?" Hermie put his cardboard 3-D Polaroid glasses on over his real ones and stared at Marc.

Marc laughed. They'd gotten the glasses in April when they went to watch *It Came from Outer Space*. Marc still had his, too. He and Eddie and Hermie wore them when they played outer space games. They'd heard another 3-D movie called *The Creature from the Black Lagoon* was coming this summer. They all hoped to get another pair of glasses.

Marc and his mother and father used to drive to Fort Smith to see the new movies long before they came to Pine Creek, since his mother loved movies almost better than anything. Mama even liked cowboy and outer space movies. But now his dad wouldn't go. They hadn't been to the movies together since January. Marc struggled to bring his thoughts back to the present, but it was hard to forget that Mama was in the sanatorium at Boonville—to forget she was sick and might never get well, might never come back home.

"I know of two battles: Pea Ridge and Prairie Grove," Marc said. As much as he liked Civil War history, his specialty was Arkansas Indians, especially the Osage. They were known for being very aggressive. Sometimes he wished he could go back through time and live with them for a few days. His relic collection helped. As he studied all the tools, weapons, and other artifacts he identified as Osage, he could imagine he was back there with them.

"I'll bet you've done nothing but read since school let out, Hermie," Marc continued. "Wasn't being promoted to sixth grade enough to make you take a few days off from studying?"

"This is not studying, Marc. I like reading this stuff."

Hermie was only ten, while Eddie and Marc were eleven, but Hermie belonged in sixth grade just as much as they did—maybe more. Eddie wasn't a great student, and Marc studied only when he had a test. He preferred reading about what he liked instead of having some teacher tell him what to study.

Where Howard Moon had flunked a grade, Hermie had skipped one. He and Marc had been best friends ever since that October when Hermie came from second grade up to third. No one but Marc had known what to say to him. "Welcome to third grade," Marc had said. "Do you like cars?" "Yeah, and airplanes," Hermie had replied. "I'm making a model of a 1926 Fokker. Want to see it?" Marc had, and that was that.

"If I read any more I'm going to go blind," Marc said, saving his news for when they found Eddie.

"Bluedog would make a good guide dog for you." Hermie snapped his fingers. Bluedog jumped on Hermie's bed, muddy feet and all.

"Boy howdy, I sure hope your mother isn't home." Marc looked around. "She'll kick us out of here."

Hermie laughed and dived into Bluedog. She and Hermie rolled and wrestled on the bed. "She's not home right now, but we can't stay here today. Mom only went to a church meeting for a couple of hours. I sure wish we could hang out at your place, like we used to."

"Well, we can't," said Marc. "And even if we could, it wouldn't be the same." Marc tackled Bluedog, hugging her warm, wiggly body. She barked in protest.

"I know." Hermie pushed his glasses up. "What do you want to do today?"

"Hey, look." Marc turned and stared at the sky. "The sun is trying to come out. I'd almost forgotten what it looked like. Let's go find Eddie. I've got some super news."

"What is it?" Hermie grabbed his jeans and favorite red T-shirt and tugged them on.

"I'll tell you later," Marc teased.

"Aw, Marc." Hermie stuck his feet in old tennis shoes and flopped on the bed to tie them. "Get off, Blue." When she leaped, Hermie pulled up his old yellow bedspread. "Mom will yell at me if I don't make my bed," he explained to the dog.

Bluedog started to get back on, until she realized the boys were heading for the kitchen. Then she trotted to catch up.

Hermie grabbed two bananas, three store-bought sweet rolls—giving Marc the last two in the package—and they ate all the way to Eddie's.

"I want to tell both of you at the same time," Marc said, eating the first roll. He started at the outside, turning it as he nibbled, then slipped the soft, gooey middle into his mouth all at once. "I have a great plan for the summer."

"You always do." Hermie stripped the first banana, tossing the peel into Gertrude Frisch's immaculate yard. Bluedog ran over and sniffed the skin, then caught up to them again. She stayed close to Hermie's hand with the squished last roll in it. "Hey, Bluedog's become a pointer," Hermie decided.

"Yeah, she points to any and all food." Marc laughed.

Eddie never encouraged them to come to his place except to pick him up. He had lived with his grandparents ever since his mother was killed in a car accident. He didn't know where his father lived. Sometimes Eddie talked about him, though. He bragged that he was sure his dad would come one day and take him out of this old folks' home.

"Hi, boys. Looking for trouble?" Pops, Eddie's grandfather, cackled with laughter that sounded more like wheezing.

"You mean Eddie?" Hermie asked, and laughed with Pops.

"When I was young, three boys your age didn't have to look far to get into some mischief."

Sometimes it was hard to remember that Pops had ever been a boy. He was as wrinkled as a walnut and complained about his arthritis all the time. He and Eddie had done some cave exploring together until a couple of years ago, but now Pops said he couldn't stand the dampness anymore.

Eddie called his house "The Mausoleum," and the name

fit. It even smelled old. Marc knocked, then went on in, knowing that Gramma Sparks couldn't hear much of anything unless it was up close to her ear.

Plug, the Sparkses' bulldog, waddled to greet them. They'd left Bluedog outside, since Plug was too old to tolerate the younger dog's playfulness.

"Hi, Plug," Hermie said, patting his head. "Is Eddie here?"

Plug was as wrinkled as Pops. He tried to wiggle a greeting, but he had arthritis, too, and didn't move very well. His full name was Sparkses' Plug, but he had little energy and no spark left.

The Sparkses' house was gloomy and full of dark antique furniture and knickknacks. As much as Marc liked Indian relics, he didn't like the collection of old stuff that Gramma Sparks prized. Chairs had white doilies on their backs and arms. Under the glass on the coffee table was a display of her button collection. The air reeked of camphor until they got to the kitchen, which smelled of chocolate and oatmeal. Eddie was lifting cookies off a baking sheet and onto a piece of waxed paper.

"Hi, Gramma Sparks," said Marc and Hermie loudly.

"Hello, boys," she said. "Would you like a cookie?"

"I wondered where you guys were." Eddie shoveled a cookie into Marc's hand and one into Hermie's. Marc tossed his cookie back and forth to cool it, then bit into the chewy sweetness.

"Hey, you make a cute cook, Eddie," Marc teased. Eddie knelt on a chair, making him almost as tall as Marc. He had a big apron tied around his chest and under his arms.

Eddie wiped one hand across his hair and ignored Marc's remark. He'd gotten awfully vain about his hair, Marc thought, since he'd started greasing it back into a ducktail with a big blob of Brylcream every day. It was a look nobody else in Pine Creek Elementary School had taken up, except Eddie who was a big Elvis Presley fan.

"I notice you didn't refuse the cookies that this cook and Gramma made, Mr. Smarty." Eddie stood up and slid out of the apron.

Marc laughed and took seconds. "The rain has stopped. Let's go outside before it starts up again."

"Go ahead, Eddie," Gramma said. "I can finish these myself. You're looking peaked from so many days inside."

Eddie didn't hesitate. He never stayed home unless he had to. Marc didn't blame him, with Pops and Gramma as old as the Civil War. Eddie grabbed a handful of cookies and followed Marc and Hermie out of the house.

"Okay, Marc, tell us," Hermie said, as soon as they were out of Pops's hearing.

"Tell us what?" Eddie slid onto his bike. Eddie's bike was a new Hawthorne tank model with an electric horn and motorcycle headlight. He had added a Hollywood goose horn and sheepskin saddle cover. It left Hermie's old Montgomery Ward model in the Dark Ages. Marc's bike wasn't much better. If they got the reward money for relics this summer, Marc could get a new one with his share.

"There's a reward poster on the bulletin board in the park," Marc said. "Fifty dollars for newly found relics. Some professor over at the university is offering the money."

"Fifty dollars! Holy Cow!" Eddie whistled low, then shouted and took off. He rode circles around Marc and Hermie, honking his goose horn. "Whoooeee, could I use fifty dollars!"

"Jumpin' Jehoshaphat!" Hermie grinned. "But my parents will make me put it in the bank."

"Where'll we find any relics like that?" Eddie said, calming down.

"Let's ride out to Mr. Daniels's place and ask him what he thinks about the reward," Marc suggested. "He might even have some suggestions for us. He used to tell my dad and me about places he thought we should look."

"Suits me." Hermie was almost always agreeable to Marc's ideas.

"Me, too." Eddie didn't argue. He pulled out a comb and smoothed back his hair on either side. "I could get a new catcher's mitt with fifty dollars."

Eddie often talked about stuff he was going to buy, as if things would make up for losing his mother. Pops and Gramma had gotten him into that habit, Marc figured. They bought him everything he wanted. Eddie hadn't mentioned his mother in a long time. And he had stopped asking Marc about his. At least Marc could hope his own mother was coming back.

He'd rather think about the fifty dollars. But he didn't want to spend the money before they got it. He did feel, though, that he and Hermie and Eddie had as good a chance of collecting the reward as anyone else in town.

3

THREE-WAY PACT

The new highway had skirted Pine Creek, taking most of the business on past and into Fort Smith, but not too many people cared. They settled for local business and the few tourists who wandered into town.

People who wanted to trade with Mr. Daniels looked him up. Everyone for miles around knew him. He ran a combination junk shop, Indian store, and pawnshop. As far as Marc, Hermie, and Eddie were concerned, Mr. Daniels had the most interesting store they'd ever seen. Marc, his dad, and Hermie had traded Indian relics with Mr. Daniels as long as Marc could remember. In fact, Mr. Daniels had given him the first tomahawk he had in his collection.

It was a large, double-bladed tomahawk, and probably worth five dollars, Marc's dad had said. Marc couldn't believe Mr. Daniels had given it to him, but now Marc knew he was just like that. If someone, especially a kid, wanted something and really didn't have the money, Mr. Daniels would usually give it to him. Sometimes he cut the price for

Marc or let him pay things out over time. He'd paid out some of his best pieces over several months. Mr. Daniels had gained a steady customer by giving Marc that good tomahawk.

One time Marc asked him how he ever made any money, giving stuff away like he did. "I make it up on the tourists, Marc," he answered. "Tourists will buy anything and usually will pay too much for it. You don't need to worry about my going broke." He laughed when he said that, and Marc decided he was right.

"Howdy, boys," Mr. Daniels greeted them from the door when he saw them lean their bikes on the fence. "Howdy, Bluedog," he said, coming out and leaning on a porch post while they walked past the boxes of mineral rocks that lined the walk leading to the wooden building. "You boys in the market for a peace pipe or some fine little bird points? I did some good trading this morning." He leaned over and scratched Bluedog.

"Howdy, Mr. Daniels," Marc said. "I'd sure like to see what you got."

"Hi, Mr. Daniels," echoed Hermie and Eddie. "So would we."

Mr. Daniels was a tall, heavy man. In fact, he looked like an older version of Hermie without the glasses. His eyes were as blue as the big turquoise ring he wore, and they sparkled when he talked to the boys. Marc always had a hard time deciding whether he was teasing or telling the truth.

They spent the next forty-five minutes unwrapping musty old newspapers from around pieces in the box on Mr. Daniels's counter. Marc shook his head, still surprised at how the old man traded. Why, he hadn't even looked at all the relics before making a deal. The box had probably come from a farmer who needed money. All the farmers in the county had relics stacked around that they'd dug up in their fields over the years. And they knew Mr. Daniels was a sucker for local people in need.

"How much did you pay for this box, Mr. Daniels?" Marc asked. "None of these pieces are very good." He'd be willing to bet that the farmer showed Mr. Daniels the bird points and hinted that the rest of the stuff was as good.

"I didn't pay much. But I'll sell them all. Most tourists don't know the difference between valuable stuff and ordinary pieces." Mr. Daniels laughed, knowing Marc thought he'd been cheated.

"Tell Hermie and Eddie about selling the bean jar, Mr. Daniels." Marc wanted to get the old man talking. He knew Mr. Daniels loved to talk even better than he liked to trade.

Mr. Daniels rolled his own cigarettes. Before he told one of his stories, he'd dig into his pocket and pull out his cigarette papers and a little pouch of tobacco. Marc liked to watch him shake just the right amount of golden-brown flakes into the paper and pull the string to close the bag with his teeth. Then he'd run his tongue along one side of the thin paper and seal the cigarette shut with his finger.

Once, Eddie had found a half pack of Camel cigarettes that Pops had lost, and he and Marc and Hermie smoked every one. All night Marc felt as if a mule had kicked him in the stomach. He wanted to die and get it over with.

So he didn't plan on smoking again, but if he ever did take up the habit, he knew he'd roll his own cigarettes. He'd already spent half a day learning to pop the head off a stick match with his thumbnail to light it. That was another of Mr. Daniels's skills. Marc had carried a box of stick matches in his pocket ever since, in case he wanted to impress someone. He wasn't much into impressing girls, but he could get a giggle out of Marcy Lee Wallace by pulling out a match and flaming it up for her. 'Course, some girls will giggle at just about anything. His mother hadn't laughed, though. She liked putting candles on the table at dinnertime. But when

Marc showed her his new trick for lighting them, she scolded, worrying he'd set the house on fire.

Marc looked at Mr. Daniels, who'd gotten comfortable in his rocking chair. Bluedog curled up beside him to snooze during story time. Holding the crumpled cigarette carefully, Mr. Daniels took a long drag. He blew the smoke out slowly and began.

"Well, after I'd had my lunch one day, I took and washed the brown glass jar my baked beans came in. I brought it out into the store and blew a little dust on it so it matched the rest of the merchandise. Not ten minutes later, a woman, dressed in real fancy clothes, mind you, came in and browsed around. I saw her looking at the jar.

" 'Is this old?' she asked, bringing it over to me. 'I don't know that much about antique glass, lady,' I said. Sometimes it pays to act dumb." Mr. Daniels took a puff of his cigarette, and his blue eyes sparkled. "Customers love to think they know more than you do about your stuff. 'I think I'll take it,' she said. 'It just might be old.' "

"How much did you charge her?" Hermie asked. Mr. Daniels had paused, leaving off that part, knowing that either Hermie or Eddie would ask. Marc already knew, of course.

"A dollar." Mr. Daniels said. "And I'd only paid seventy-five cents for it when it was full of beans."

They all laughed. Bluedog woke up and barked to get in on the conversation. Marc wanted to tell Mr. Daniels *he* was full of beans. His mother used to say that to him, meaning he was pulling her leg. She was always easy to fool; she'd believe anything. His dad always called her a city girl. He loved to tease her, too.

"We've got to go, Mr. Daniels." Suddenly Marc needed to ride his bike really fast. Why couldn't he stop thinking about his mother?

Hermie raised his eyebrows up and down, up and down,

to remind Marc he hadn't asked about the reward poster. Eddie poked his finger halfway through Marc's back.

"You boys see the sign out front?" Mr. Daniels asked, before Marc had a chance to question him about where to look for relics. He took one last drag on the cigarette and ground out the stub on his concrete floor. "You three might as well try for the reward."

Marc looked at Hermie and Eddie in surprise and then looked up at the porch post. Sure enough, they'd passed right by a sign identical to the one hanging in the park. Then Marc remembered that Mr. Daniels had been leaning on that post when they came up to the store. He thought he'd saved a surprise for the boys until they got ready to leave.

"If we found a grave, who would it belong to?" Marc asked as the four of them read the sign again.

"Whoever owned the property, silly," said Eddie. "Isn't that right, Mr. Daniels?"

"Yes, unless it was in the state park. Then I figure it'd go to a museum or the university so they could study it. I don't reckon there's much left to find these days, but it'd be fun to look."

Mr. Daniels had been digging Indian relics since he was a boy. That's how he got started in the business. Marc liked to listen to him tell about those days. The farmers would call him when they plowed up stuff, and he'd go over and dig.

"I figure it'd be easy to find some good stuff if we took time to look," Eddie said, when Mr. Daniels went back inside.

"You heard Mr. Daniels, Eddie," Marc said. "He's an expert, and *he* doesn't think it'd be easy. You think you'll be good at everything before you try it. Remember the pool table that Mr. Ellis put in the back of the drugstore? He said we could play when it wasn't busy. Well, you said you'd get it in no time."

"Aw, horse pucky. I'll get the hang of it soon. Mr. Daniels

has just gotten too old to get out and look for relics himself, so he says there's not any more good stuff."

Eddie might have had a point, but Marc wasn't going to waste time arguing with him. Sometimes Marc thought Eddie liked to argue better than anything else—the same way Mr. Daniels liked to tell stories. But Marc got tired of Eddie's bragging.

"I hope we aren't going to spend all summer digging around in the woods," said Hermie.

"You just want to spend it digging in the library, in a bunch of dusty old books," Eddie accused Hermie.

"Hey, it sounds as if we're going to spend all summer fighting," Marc said. "What else have we got to do except look for relics? Think how exciting it'll be if we find something."

"Let's make it a contest. We'll see which one of us can collect the reward," suggested Eddie.

"I think we should work together and share the reward." Marc figured splitting up would take the fun out of it. Being realistic, he knew all they'd probably find would be some arrowheads or some pottery shards. A big find these days was rare. But that's why the reward was so high. "Whatever one of us finds, we'll share and split the reward three ways. Deal?" Marc put out his hand.

Hermie reached out immediately.

Eddie frowned and hesitated. "Only if we're together when we find it. If I stumble over a grave when I'm alone, I'm not going to share it."

Eddie and Hermie looked at Marc. "That's fair enough," Marc agreed. He was certain that wouldn't happen.

Eddie took Marc's hand and Hermie laid his on top of theirs. Under the reward poster, the three of them shook. Then they crossed their hearts and pulled a finger across their throats, swearing they'd never tell about the pact.

4

BLUEDOG'S RABBIT

Bluedog barked, saying she wanted in on their deal. Marc hugged her. "Yes, you too, Blue," he said, laughing. "You can help dig."

"And we'll buy you the biggest bone you ever saw if you find anything," Hermie said in agreement.

"Let's begin looking this afternoon," Marc suggested as they jumped on their bikes and started back toward town. "It could rain again tomorrow."

"I'm hungry." Hermie puffed as he pumped to keep up with Marc and Eddie. "I don't want to go exploring until after lunch."

Marc was hungry, too, but he didn't want to go back home for lunch. He hesitated. Hermie knew what he was thinking. Marc didn't tell Hermie too many of his feelings, but Hermie was good at figuring out what was going on in people's minds—especially Marc's. Marc guessed that was why they'd been friends for so long. They didn't always have to talk about how they felt.

"Come eat at my house, both of you," Hermie invited, after looking at his watch. "Mom will be gone again now. She's working afternoons at the beauty shop this summer."

"Thanks, Herm. If you're sure your mom won't mind." Marc knew that even if Mrs. Harrington wasn't home, she would know three boys and a dog had eaten there.

"She will, but I don't care." Hermie led the way.

Bluedog followed them inside at Hermie's, but Marc made her sit on the sleeping porch. She scooted forward until she could see the boys in the kitchen. Then she put her head on her paws and took on her sad look.

"She never gives up, does she?" Hermie took peanut butter and a loaf of Wonder Bread out of the cupboard. From the fridge he got his mom's homemade muscadine jam.

Marc's mouth watered at the thought of the sweetly tart taste of muscadines. He smeared his bread generously and washed down two sandwiches with ice-cold milk.

"Let's take a snack with us." Hermie found his day pack, khaki-colored and crumpled like an old paper bag.

"That looks like a pack Pops might have carried in World War I," Eddie teased, as Hermie tossed in apples, cookies, and a Hershey bar each.

Hermie laughed. "Maybe it is. My dad got it at the Army Surplus."

Marc was glad Mrs. Harrington kept plenty of food in the house. At his place he either had to remind his dad to go grocery shopping or else do it himself, adding it to their bill at the City Market. Marc's mother had always kept the pantry overflowing. He'd found out a lot of things that she did for them after she left. Things he liked—things he'd always taken for granted.

They crossed the south side of the square again to get to the old highway that led to the bluffs. Marc soon wished they'd taken the back streets when Howard Moon appeared and skidded his bike right in front of them, forcing them to stop.

"Where are you all going? Hunting for Indian relics, by any chance?" Mooney grinned.

Eddie could never keep his mouth shut. "None of your beeswax, Mooney." Marc kept telling Eddie that ignoring Mooney worked best, but Eddie had a short fuse and a big mouth.

"What if I make it my business, Greasehead?" Mooney dodged in front of Marc. Marc had already started to go around him.

"We're going out to the bluffs to look for arrowheads, Mooney," Marc said. "Want to come along?" Sometimes the truth worked best.

"Naw. You think a handful of arrowheads is going to win that reward, Schaller? You've got to think bigger than that. Let me know when you're going for the big find. Then I'll tag along with the kiddies here." Mooney nodded toward Hermie and Eddie.

Eddie was eleven in November, but he was so small people sometimes mistook him for ten. He'd come to Arkansas from a California school. The teachers found he'd had all the fourth grade books before, so they let him try fifth. He'd made it through, just barely. Hermie and Marc had to help him a lot with math. Marc never worried about running around with two guys younger than he was. Hermie and Eddie were certainly better company than Mooney.

"That guy's a pile of horse pucky. He makes me want to punch him out." Eddie ran his hands down both sides of his head, smoothing his hair. Then he stood on his pedals and pumped to get going fast.

"Why don't you ignore him? I keep telling you that works best." The chain on Marc's bike slipped, and he had to pedal a lot to make it catch. *I'm the one who needs that money for a new bike,* he thought.

"I can't ignore him. What if he'd come with us? Why'd you invite him, Marc?" Eddie circled back to where Marc was trying to get some traction.

"He'd never want to tag along with us," explained Hermie, who understood Marc's tactics. "Unless we didn't want him to, or he thought we'd found something good."

"Hey!" Mooney yelled. He was following them. Had he changed his mind? "If you ever want to get rid of that funny-looking dog, Schaller, I have a friend who runs a freak show." Mooney cackled with laughter, zipped in front of them, then took off back to town, singing, "How much is that doggie in the window?" as he disappeared.

"Very funny," Eddie shouted after him.

Mooney knew how attached Marc was to Bluedog—how she went every place he went, except to school. He figured if he couldn't get to Marc any other way, he'd try making fun of his dog. And it almost worked.

Marc knew Bluedog was funny-looking, but she was the smartest dog he'd ever known. His dad had said so, too, when they got her. A man who'd needed some insurance had traded Bluedog for the first premium. She had funny markings even as a puppy, but she learned every trick Marc could think of in record time.

Then Marc nearly lost her. She got sick, and the vet didn't know what it was. Marc sat up with her day and night, making her eat one bite at a time out of his hand. He talked to her, begged her not to die. The vet said Marc saved her life. Then he told Marc the Chinese people believe that when you save someone's life, you're responsible for them forever. Marc had been especially close to Bluedog ever since. Sometimes he knew how she was feeling, and she always knew how Marc was feeling. His mother called them twins—said twins sometimes didn't even have to talk to each other, they understood without words or just talked with their minds. "Twin to a dog," she'd teased Marc.

The man had called her an Australian Blue, a type of sheepdog found in Australia. There was a layer of dark hair under Blue's short white coat, causing her to have a bluish tint all over. She had black spots, and her eyes were a funny light brown. Bluedog's extra-long legs added to her odd look, but that made her the jumper she was. Marc loved to see her sail out and over a low fence, chasing her ball.

Bluedog had one fault, as far as Marc was concerned. She had a passion for rabbits.

Now she ran ahead of their bikes for a time, anticipating the fun she was going to have in the woods. As soon as they stopped riding, though, she was off and running through the woods. First one way, then another, nose to the ground, hunting fresh rabbit scent.

"Look at that fool dog, Marc." Eddie laughed. "She'd never be any good herding sheep now. She wouldn't have time."

"Not that we'd trade her, but maybe there's a job for a dog who herds rabbits." Hermie laughed at Bluedog, too, but Marc knew both he and Eddie really loved her.

"Let's hide our bikes," Marc suggested, picking his up and setting it down in a small thicket of shrub oak that was thick with new leaves and full of water droplets.

Marc's action frightened a rabbit who'd taken up hiding in the thicket. The cottontail flashed across the clearing ahead of Bluedog. She tore after it.

"You could say thanks," Marc yelled after the streak of blue and gray. He laughed. She *was* funny.

"What would she do if she caught one?" Eddie asked, setting his bike alongside Marc's.

"I think it would scare her to death," Marc answered. "Let's go down to the river. Something may have washed up in the rains."

"Come back, Blue. We're going this way," Hermie called

to Bluedog as he swung his knapsack onto his back, pushed up his glasses, and took the trail that led down to the bluffs and the river.

Eddie and Marc followed Hermie, but Marc held back a little, calling to Bluedog. She seemed obsessed with this particular rabbit.

They walked along in silence, their sneakers pad, pad, padding on the soft earth, still soggy from the rain. The oaks and hickories overhead were green and lush, creating a shady tunnel as they headed downhill through deep forest. Verbenas were covered with pink blossoms that perfumed the damp air. Slender dogwoods had finished their spring blooming. Now their green leaves blended into the approaching summer. Here it was, all around them, at last— the freedom Marc had craved all through May while they were stuck in school. Best yet, the sun kept peeking out, promising dryer days.

Watching for poison ivy, they ignored the other bushes that slapped against their jeans, splattering water on their legs.

Soon Marc realized that Bluedog wasn't catching up to them. There was no muffled thump-thump-thump behind them. No huffing and puffing. No Bluedog crashing cross-country taking canine shortcuts.

Marc stopped. Listened. "Bluedog! Bluedog—come on, now. Bluedog! Wait up, guys."

"Dumb dog." Eddie shuffled back to where Marc waited.

"We'd better go back." Hermie sounded worried.

"She knows these woods better than we do." Marc felt frustrated. He didn't want to go back. It'd been three weeks since he'd been in the woods. He had sat in the classroom imagining the feel of the river's lazy, warm water on his bare feet. He wanted to wander around at the foot of the bluffs. He'd found arrowheads there before, especially after a lot of rain, and they'd had high water all spring. Anything could have washed up. Excitement filled Marc's stomach, and he felt as wiggly as Bluedog when she knew they were going someplace.

Marc sighed and turned around. "Bluedog, where are you!" he yelled.

They kept calling as they retraced their steps, impatiently, all the way back to where they'd hidden the bikes. Then they walked in the direction that Bluedog had first chased the rabbit.

"She wouldn't go far away from us," Marc said. "Even for a rabbit. She always keeps up."

"Well, then, where is she?" Eddie stood still and listened again. His patience had run out.

Marc listened, too, but he had a strange feeling. Bluedog never did anything like this, never got this far from him. But the fact was, she was gone. Something was wrong. Bluedog had completely disappeared.

5

THE CAVE

"I think she's in trouble," Marc said, sensing Bluedog was frightened, but not telling Eddie and Hermie how he knew. They would think he was crazy if he told them that he and Bluedog were like twins. How many people can read dog thoughts? But Marc knew his feelings were true. Bluedog was trying to tell him she needed him.

He got more and more scared, but all he knew to do was to keep looking and calling out. They searched the area methodically, circling farther and farther away from the bikes, fighting the wet, bushy undergrowth. When their route met the road on one side, they concentrated on the other. They would soon run out of space on that side, too, since there was a drop-off to the river below.

"We could sure use a machete," Hermie said, as he pushed aside verbena branches, shaking water droplets, sweetly perfumed, onto the three of them.

"We're going to be lucky if we don't get covered with poison ivy." Eddie jerked limbs from in front of his face, letting them slap back at Marc, who caught them, ignoring Eddie's mood. His own anger had dissolved into worry. Bluedog was his best friend, and he had to find her.

A hackberry branch slapped his cheek. He barely noticed the stinging. *I'm here, I'm here,* Bluedog kept saying to him. *Where?* Marc felt like shouting, but Hermie and Eddie would freak out if he went around talking to Blue when she wasn't there.

Finally the sound of barking reached his ears, but it seemed to come from far off. It had a funny, hollow sound as if she were in a tunnel. "Bluedog?" Marc shouted.

"Over this way!" Hermie heard it, too.

A huge outcropping of rocks bordered the edge of the drop-off to the river. They made their way in that direction, calling and looking in all possible hiding spaces. Maybe she was tangled in blackberry vines. But no Bluedog.

Marc held to the rocks and looked over the bluff, half expecting to see Bluedog standing on a ledge looking up at him. Could she have fallen off? She wasn't that dumb, but if she was excited about the rabbit she might have been careless.

"Bluedog?" Marc called out again.

"Down here, Marc, down here! Jumpin' Jehoshaphat! Come and look!" Hermie shouted.

"It's—it's a cave," Marc said. It had to be. They could hear Bluedog right under them, but they couldn't see her.

They searched the rocks until they found the small hole. All around it the dirt was loose, as if Bluedog had tried to hold on to the edge.

"Holy Cow! I knew we'd find something good this summer." Eddie grinned ear to ear, taking all the credit, as if he'd stumbled into the cave himself.

"Jeez, this is something you only read about in books," said Hermie, peering into the darkness.

"Listen, a guy found Mammoth Cave in Kentucky when he chased a rabbit into a hole. It's not impossible." Marc lay down beside Hermie and tried to see inside, but it was pitch black past the opening. He heard little whining noises. "It's okay, Bluedog, it's okay," he said into the darkness.

"You think this is that old cave people talk about all the time?" asked Eddie. "If it is, we may be famous for finding it."

"Bluedog found it," Marc reminded Eddie.

"There are probably caves throughout these bluffs that no one has found." Hermie wasn't an explorer, but he read about everything.

There was an old story around town that a large cave existed in the area. But no one could remember where it was. Mr. Daniels said he remembered searching for it when he was a boy. His dad had talked about it.

Marc laughed, partly out of relief for finding Blue, partly out of excitement. "She must have chased that rabbit right in there, like Alice down the rabbit hole. Bluedog, are you all right?" He lay on his stomach and shouted through the hole, almost hidden with long grasses and a patch of honeysuckle.

Bluedog barked an answer. It was obvious that she was a long way down. "Oooof, oooof," her voice echoed.

"Dumb dog," Eddie said, but this time with some pride in his voice.

"How are we going to get her out?" Hermie asked.

"How are we going to get ourselves in? That's the question. Boy howdy, a cave to explore." Marc's mind raced. It would take ropes. He wondered if his dad would help.

"You sure we want to go in? Let's get Bluedog out and forget we ever found this place." Hermie had never pretended to be an explorer. He preferred to get his excitement from reading about someone else's adventures.

"Not go in? You must be kidding. Of course we're going in." Eddie was ready to slide right down the hole like Bluedog had done.

"It could be something incredible, like Crystal Cave." Marc raised up and looked around. "I wonder who owns this land."

"It's close to the river, so it's probably part of the state park." Hermie leaned on a rock, waiting for Marc to make a decision about Bluedog.

"I guess it doesn't matter who owns this land right now. I know Bluedog doesn't care." Marc lay back down and spoke into the hole. "Stay, Blue. Stay right there. We'll be back in a little while. We have to go get some rope."

"Think she'll stay?" Eddie asked, as they headed for their bikes.

"Sure. Where would she go? She can't see any better than we could down there with no light. I wonder if we can get her out." Marc turned the problem over and over in his mind. He'd have to go in and help her. No way could they toss a rope down there and say, "Bluedog, climb up this rope." He almost smiled at the idea.

"Would your dad—?"

"I don't know." Marc stopped Hermie's question. He had no idea if his father would help them. Marc could never predict his moods lately, and he felt uncomfortable around him. Surely his dad wouldn't want Bluedog to be left there, but since he didn't seem to care about Marc anymore, maybe he wouldn't care about Bluedog either. "Let's go get my ropes. I think this is up to us." Marc decided not to approach his dad. They'd get Bluedog out themselves.

They scrambled to their feet, and Marc looked back to make sure he could recognize the spot again. It was totally hidden and, except for a couple of bent-over branches, looked undisturbed. It was far enough from the path to the river that no one would happen by and find it or hear Blue-dog if she barked again. She didn't bark often, just when she was awfully excited or wanted something. Marc knew she wanted out of that hole really badly, but it was going to take some time. He sure hoped he and Hermie and Eddie could manage it alone.

6

TROUBLE WITH MOONEY AGAIN

Marc's house was an insurance agency in the front, with the living space in the back. It sat on the northeast corner of the square. He had always liked living right in town. That way he didn't miss much. The boys turned their bikes into the driveway, skidded to a stop, and jumped off beside the back fence.

Their Chevy was home, but there were two cars parked in front, too. Marc hoped they were both customers who would keep his dad busy. They only needed time enough to get in, get some gear, and get out. Marc figured if his dad didn't see him, he wouldn't ask any questions. In fact, these days, Marc felt that if his father wasn't forced to see him occasionally at meals, he wouldn't remember Marc existed. And there were times when that was okay. This was definitely one of those times.

Marc had never done any cave exploring on his own. If his father did happen into the back of the house and see them carrying ropes, he would ask questions. Marc cautioned

Eddie and Hermie to be quiet. He wasn't going to leave Bluedog in that cave all night.

They got into Marc's room, into his closet, and found the coils of rope he and his dad used for climbing when they went spelunking. Before Mama got sick, they had explored only a couple of caves where they'd had to do any technical climbing. But since January, Marc's dad had lost interest in everything. All their equipment was stored either in the back of Marc's closet or in the shed outside. Marc picked up his big three-cell flashlight, hoping the batteries were still good. He tested it. Yep, seemed strong.

"If we're going down there anyway, we might as well explore some—don't you agree, Hermie?" Marc was getting goose bumps as he handled the ropes and thought ahead.

"Wait, Marc." Hermie put up both hands. "You know I've never done this before. I don't think I want to do it now. I'm not built for wiggling around through underground tunnels in rock."

"If you get stuck, you'll have to stay until you lose weight." Eddie laughed.

"A good reason for dieting, you have to admit," Marc added.

"I don't want to go on a diet," Hermie said.

"I won't go anywhere you can't follow," Marc promised. He hoisted the rope to his shoulder, putting his light and some candles in his backpack. Then they tiptoed out the back door. Marc looked into the backyard. The memory of Bluedog there, wiggling desperately, made him even firmer in his resolve to get her out of the hole and bring her home today.

"Shouldn't we tell someone where we're going?" Hermie suggested as they reached their bikes and took off without Marc's father seeing them. "Isn't that the safe thing to do?"

"We won't go that far into the cave today," Marc decided.

Hermie was right. They should leave a note. But Marc didn't want to. He wanted this to be his cave until he got ready to share it. Maybe his dad would feel proud of a son who discovered a new cave. Maybe this would make him pay attention to Marc like he used to. He'd say, "Marc, I need a guide through your cave. Will you take me in?" Marc would forgive him for forgetting he had a son. He'd say, "Sure, Dad, no charge."

Out on the street, they ran out of luck. There was Howard Moon again, and his buddy, Otis. Otis Kruger was a tall, skinny guy who looked like a skeleton barely covered with flesh. You could practically see bones moving under his skin. And his skin was white, except where it was pasted together with freckles.

Darn the luck. Didn't Mooney and Kruger have anything better to do than hang around in town?

"Hey, you guys back already? What are you fixing to do now?" Mooney saw the ropes. There was no way they could hide them.

"We're going to practice rappelling over on the bluffs," Marc said, hoping Mooney believed him. There was one good limestone face where climbers practiced near the river.

"Why don't I believe you, Schaller? You wouldn't lie to your old buddy Moon, would you?"

Marc had never been buddies with Howard Moon, and he didn't plan to start a friendship now. "Maybe you think I'd lie because you know how much of a liar you are, Mooney." Marc motioned for Hermie and Eddie, and they started pedaling up the highway, slowly, as if they had all day. But they didn't, and a slow pace was frustrating. It must be getting near three o'clock. If they stayed out past dinnertime one of their parents would surely ask questions.

"Don't look now, Marc, but you didn't discourage them." Eddie scowled. "I told you ignoring them wouldn't work."

"What'll we do?" Hermie looked to Marc for an answer. Mooney and Otis followed at a leisurely pace.

The rope Marc carried was heavy. He didn't want to lug it all the way down to the river, pretend they were going to climb, then lug it back. Besides, they didn't have that much time. But Marc wasn't going to let Mooney and Otis in on the cave. He didn't know what might come of it, but it was their discovery. Well, actually, it was Bluedog's.

"Let's lose them," he decided.

"How? We can't get that far ahead."

"We'll split up. You take off through the woods just around this curve, Hermie. Eddie and I might be able to outride them. Hide your bike and make your way to the cave. We'll get there when we can. But whatever you do, don't let anyone see you."

"I'll try," Hermie promised.

They rounded the curve. Hermie spun out and fell into the gravel on the shoulder of the road. That wasn't in the plan, but Marc hoped Hermie's spill was as good as hiding. He pumped to catch up with Eddie.

Sure enough, Mooney yelled, "What's the matter, Hermie-child? Can't you keep up?" Mooney laughed, but he and Otis kept following Eddie and Marc. Hermie could make good his escape.

Marc pulled ahead and whispered the plan to Eddie. They took off as if it was the race of the year. The mountain road was curvy, winding around and around. They hustled up the next climb. At full speed, they flew down the other side of the hill. Rounding a curve, Marc glanced back.

"We're hidden for a few seconds," Marc called to Eddie. "Let's jump."

Marc's hands slipped on the black rubber handlebar grips. He could feel the sweat pouring down his back.

"Now!" he yelled. He zipped onto a grassy verge, leaping

off his bike. The coil of rope swung, slapping his waist, and he nearly fell. He pulled his bike into a hidden pocket of trees and looked back. Eddie wasn't with him. He'd altered the plan. He'd kept going as bait for Mooney and Otis. Eddie was the best rider. His bike was new. Maybe his plan would work. But this split them up three ways.

Voices told Marc that Mooney knew he was their leader. He and Otis had stopped, at least long enough to decide what to do, who to follow.

Taking advantage of their indecision, Marc pushed his bike out of the hiding place. He was grateful for the wet ground that softened the noise of his escape. But it would also leave easy tracks to follow. Lifting his bike, he took off into the brush. He swished downhill, making a path where none existed. He ignored the briars that tore at his jeans and snatched at the rope and the bike—blackberries in the fall, a nuisance now.

He got a small break. A tiny stream with a bed of rocks cut north and downhill. He ran his bike through the water, soaking his shoes and pants to the knee. But it was easier than trying to get through the brush. The stream would also hide tracks and any mashing down of grass or undergrowth. A good Indian could still follow him easily, but he hoped Mooney was lazy enough to give up.

The woods took Marc in like an old friend. It was cool and quiet. Before long he left the stream and slid his bike behind a huge rock that was surrounded by young hickory trees. Even if Mooney found Marc now, he wouldn't find the cave. Marc would laugh, and say, "I give." For a minute he collapsed beside the rock, taking deep breaths of the air, scented by crushed mint. His clothes were so wet he felt as if he were in a sweat lodge. Mosquitoes whined around his head. He swatted them silently.

He crouched, his back against the rock, until the woods got noisy again, telling him no one had followed. A hermit thrush warbled its robin-like melody. A mockingbird landed on top of the rock, cocked its head, and looked down at Marc. Then it took off, startled by a human visitor. Marc smiled and knew he had escaped successfully. Now if he could only find his way to the cave from here, he was in business.

He waited another fifteen minutes for good measure. A skink sensed him, froze on the rocks and wet leaves, then scurried away at lizard speed.

When he stood, shaking the needle pricks from his foot where it had gone to sleep, he studied his hiding place carefully. If he was going to leave his bike here, he wanted to be sure he could find it. He'd go back up the stream and mark where it started.

Marc cursed Mooney again. Why'd he have to complicate Marc's life like this? He knew he'd never find the cave if he cut cross-country. He'd have to risk going closer to the road and following it to where the path to the bluffs started downward. If Mooney was waiting there, they'd never get Bluedog out before dark.

It took him a half hour of tracing and retracing his steps, getting his bearings and hiking carefully, before he made his way safely to the cave entrance. The rope felt like a coil of braided lead on his shoulder. He was wet through. Maybe it would have been easier to carry the rope down to the river, wait out Mooney's patience, then take it back to the cave. Too late now to make that decision. Marc sighed and looked around. Hermie and Eddie were no place in sight.

"Where've you been?" Eddie appeared like a ghost from behind the clump of rocks.

"How'd you get ahead of me?" Marc asked.

"Those guys gave up easily," Eddie boasted. "I hid and waited them out, then rode my bike back to the cutoff."

"Me too." Hermie stepped from behind the other side of the rock. "You have trouble?"

Marc thought of all the trouble he'd gone to, pretending half a tribe of hostile Osage were behind him. All he could do was shake his head and grin. "Some."

"Bluedog has given up on you, too." Eddie lay down and spoke to the dog. "We could have had her out by now."

Bluedog whined and whimpered, tired of the dark and the isolation. Marc spoke into the hole. "We're coming, Blue. We're coming, hang on."

He looked for a place to attach the rope, not wanting Eddie or Hermie to have to support his weight if they could figure out another plan. There were no trees big enough, but Marc decided one of the rocks was secure. Looping the rope around it, he tied a knot he knew wouldn't slip. Then he tested it by pulling with all his strength.

"Why don't you belay me?" Marc said to Eddie. They hadn't climbed together, but he knew if Eddie hadn't learned this from Pops, he'd catch on to the technique fast. He showed both Hermie and Eddie how to loop the rope around their waists and let it run through their hands, playing it out a bit at a time, while Marc climbed down. If they were going to start spelunking without Marc's dad or Pops, they might as well get used to working as a team.

"I'm ready." Marc held onto the rope that was circled around his waist, then threaded through his hands. He slid through the narrow opening in the ground and found that it widened out almost immediately. He was able to place his feet on the side wall and half walk, half slide down, until there were some rocks to hold onto. His body blocked the light from above, so he had to pretty much feel his way down. He hadn't worn his helmet or brought his lamp, and his flashlight was in his pack so he could have his hands free. He could hear Bluedog jumping and whimpering, her toenails scratching on the cave floor.

The temperature dropped. The cave felt damp and musty

even near the air hole. But the smell sent a shiver of excitement over Marc. He wondered how long it'd been since anyone had been in this cave—had humans ever been in it? Was this one of the many undiscovered caves in the Arkansas hills that people often talked about?

When he reached the bottom, Marc was almost licked to death. "Thought I'd abandoned you, didn't you, Blue, old girl?" He hugged his dog and held her until she stopped shivering and wiggling. "Now to tackle the problem of getting you out of here," he whispered in her ear. She sloshed his face again as if to say, "Thank you."

He looked at the small circle of light overhead. It was about twenty-five feet to the top. Luckily Bluedog hadn't broken a leg, but he imagined she had slid at least part of the way, since the ledge slanted off instead of dropping straight down. He looked at the rope, then at Bluedog. Darn! He hadn't been thinking ahead. He couldn't tie the rope around the dog and expect it to stay while Hermie and Eddie lifted her to the top. Bluedog would slip right out of a loop.

"What's wrong?" Hermie shouted down, wondering what was taking Marc so long.

"I need your shirt, Hermie," Marc shouted back. "To make a sling for Bluedog."

"Why mine? Take yours off."

"I'm already freezing down here." Marc shivered. Even if they did have time today, he'd never last in the cave for long. He was sweaty and wet from the stream and the bushes he'd crawled through, and he hadn't brought enough warm clothing or anything dry to change into.

Hermie's shirt, smelling sweaty, hit him in the face. Marc laughed. He had been half teasing Hermie, hardly hoping he could talk him out of his favorite T-shirt. Quickly he tied the rope to the bunched-up top of the shirt, hoping it would hold.

After slipping the shirt onto Bluedog and centering it around her middle, Marc tested the sling. The T-shirt would probably stretch a lot, but he thought it would hold. He hoped Blue wouldn't wiggle and jump around, or she still might fall out.

Bluedog didn't know why Marc was doing such a funny thing to her, but she went along with it, licking him in the eye.

"I know, you're glad I'm here, Blue. I know. Stop telling me. Okay, pull her up!" Marc called to Hermie and Eddie. "Slowly. Stay, Bluedog, stay."

The swinging motion frightened Bluedog, and she was no more than four feet off the ground when she started to wiggle and bark. She yipped, stretched, and slid right out of the shirt. Ker-plunk, right at Marc's feet she landed. She leaped and jumped, thinking she'd done something smart.

"No, girl. No." Marc felt defeated. But if she'd stay still, it would work. It had to.

"She didn't like it." Hermie stated the obvious.

"She doesn't like wearing your sweaty shirt," Eddie called, teasing.

Marc put the T-shirt around Blue's belly again, keeping it as wide as he could, stretching it from her front legs to her back.

"Take it up just a little at a time," Marc called. "I'll talk her through it."

Hermie started to reel in the rope again. Again Bluedog rose from the floor. Marc steadied her. "Good girl, Blue. Now, stay, stay—please." Hermie pulled again. Marc talked some more. "Easy, girl, easy. It's okay."

"Come up with her," Eddie suggested.

"Too much weight. I think she's okay this time. "Stay, girl, stay. Elevator going up. Freedom at the top. Stay."

She was more patient this time. Maybe she sensed this was

not a game. Marc sent her messages, all the way up, both out loud and in his mind. *Steady, girl, steady.*

At the top, Hermie helped Bluedog back through the hole and then retrieved his shirt. "My shirt will never be the same."

"Ugh, doggie B.O.," Eddie teased. His voice echoed as it reached Marc.

"If you want to know the truth, Hermie, Bluedog didn't want to put it on. I wasn't going to say anything," Marc yelled.

"Are you coming back up?" Eddie called. "Or should I come down?"

Marc hesitated, wanting to take off through the cave now that Blue was safe. Even a little way would give him some idea of what they'd found. But he knew it must be nearly five o'clock. It would take them a while to get home. Just one question about where they'd been would be enough to spoil their chances of returning.

"I'm coming up," Marc decided. "I'm freezing, and it's too late today to explore."

He took the rope that Hermie threw back down, and scrambled up the slope. Dirt and rocks slid as he climbed, spilling into the quiet of the cave—the cave that waited silently for them, inviting them back.

"Can you all come back with me tomorrow?" Marc asked as soon as he reached the top and flopped onto the grass. The sun was behind the trees, but the air was warm. It felt wonderful after the cold of the cave.

"I'm not sure I want to, Marc," Hermie said. "In case I never told you, I hate caves. I hate the idea of caves. I hate the dark. I used to be afraid of the dark."

"You're not still afraid of the dark, are you, Hermie?" Eddie grinned.

Hermie hesitated. He looked at Marc, then Eddie. He

looked at Bluedog, who wiggled all over and licked Hermie's ear. He looked at the blue, blue summer sky, rain only a memory. "Yes. I cannot tell a lie. I'm still afraid of the dark."

"Then it's time you got over it." Marc coiled the rope and flung it over his shoulder. "And tomorrow is as good a day as any."

7

MARC'S MOTHER

When Marc got home, his father had an idea that changed his plans for the next day's exploration. "Where've you been, boy?" His dad was stirring up a box of macaroni and cheese.

"I—I rode farther than I realized on my bike." Marc gave his dad part of an answer. "I was with Hermie and Eddie."

His father frowned, but Marc didn't say any more. After leaving the cave, it had taken him a long time to find his bike. That surprised him, since he knew the woods by the river so well. But when they'd escaped from Mooney, he hadn't paid much attention to landmarks.

Hermie and Eddie had ridden on back to town without him. Hermie said his mom would ground him if he was late for supper. There was one rule at his house: Everyone had to be home for the evening meal. Eddie was too excited to sit and wait for Marc, and he didn't want to help him hunt.

"You lost your bike, you find it." He'd laughed and ridden off.

"Can I help with supper?" Marc brought his mind back

to the kitchen and smiled as Bluedog drank a bowl of water, lay down, and was immediately asleep. She hadn't wanted to help Marc look for his bike either, but she went along. She'd had an exhausting adventure.

"You can slice some tomatoes," his dad answered.

Marc watched him stir the gummy mess. The kitchen smelled all cheesy. He hoped his father would remember to put the pan in the sink to soak, since Marc was in charge of dishes.

Marc's dad was tall and blond like his son. He was wiry, but he looked thinner than Marc could ever remember. He looked worried, and it seemed as if he never smiled anymore.

"Did you get a letter from Mama?" Her letters always made his dad get even quieter—a hopeless look on his face.

"Yes. She says she misses us. She's lonely, boy. I'm going to take the day off tomorrow and go over there, instead of waiting until Sunday. I want you to go with me."

"Tomorrow?" Marc had planned on going to visit Mama Sunday. He had his heart set on going deeper into the cave the next day. But he wanted to see his mother, too. "Sure, Dad. You know I want to go."

His father put the pan on the table on a hot pad instead of emptying it into a bowl or onto their plates. Marc remembered the candles that had gotten him in trouble when he lit them with his show-off match trick. Suddenly he wished Mama were here to fuss at him. Here to set the table with flowers and candles.

"Dad, are we ever going spelunking again?" Marc was getting tired of the silence. He'd try to get his father to talk to him.

"I don't know, boy. You know I don't have any spare time. The money is tight with your mother's bills, and I need to keep my mind on my work."

Marc thought if his dad had been out hunting clients, or keeping his mind on work, he might go along with the excuse. But many times when he'd come into the office in the front of the house, he'd found his dad staring into space. Unopened letters were piling up on his desk, and Marc had been there once when a client had stopped to complain about no one coming to check on a claim.

It got quiet again, and Marc switched on the radio. The Crewcuts were singing "Sha-boom," one of his favorite songs, but he felt his mind drifting before it was over.

Something kept Marc from telling his father about the new cave. He knew what it was. He was afraid his dad would say he couldn't explore it alone. And if he wouldn't go with them, that meant Marc would have to forget they'd found it. He knew he couldn't do that, and Eddie wouldn't—Eddie would go in alone.

Marc decided right then he was going in, no one was going to stop him. But he was going to be careful. He was no chicken, but there were about a thousand ways you could get into trouble exploring a cave; also, he was responsible for Hermie, who'd never done any exploring.

There was another reason Marc kept the cave secret, too. It was time he started doing things on his own. He didn't always need his father along as if he were a little kid.

Marc watched as his dad picked at his food, then got up, taking his half-full plate and scraping it into the trash can. He didn't even think about Bluedog; leftovers were her favorite. As Marc finished and took his plate to the sink, he heard the television set come on in the living room. Only a few people in Pine Creek had television sets. His father had bought this one for Mama at Christmas. She hadn't gotten to watch it for long before she had to leave. Now, every night after dinner, his dad turned it on and watched until after the ten o'clock news. Sometimes Marc wondered if he really watched or if he just used it as an excuse to sit and do nothing—an excuse not to think about what had happened to their family, which had once been so happy.

Running hot water into the sink, Marc watched the soap turn into foamy bubbles. He thought about Mama way off in that place, missing them as much as they missed her.

It was January when the doctor decided the cough Mama had wasn't just a cough. He had run some tests and diagnosed tuberculosis. Marc had hardly heard of it, except when he read the name in his health book at school. He'd looked up the word again when Mama told him about it. What he really wanted to know was what no one seemed to want to tell him. Could Mama die of it?

Then she'd told Marc she couldn't stay at home anymore. She didn't want to risk his or Dad's catching it. And she needed rest and full-time care to get over it.

It had snowed the day they took her to the sanatorium at Boonville. Marc would never forget that trip back home over slick highways, the world as cold as his insides. After that his dad hadn't said a word for three days.

At least Boonville wasn't that far from where they lived. They could go to visit Mama. It was hard to leave her there every time, but Marc had started to get used to it. Mama was so cheerful when they were there. If she ever did any crying or complaining, she did it after they left.

When Marc finished the dishes he walked quietly into the office part of the house. Quickly he dialed Hermie's number. "Hermie," he said, after his mother had called him to the phone. "I have to postpone tomorrow. I'm sure that will break your heart."

"It sure does, Marc. For how long? About two years?"

"Don't you wish. Where's your sense of adventure, Hermie?"

"I guess I lost it out there in the woods today. Sorry. I'll look for it while you and Eddie explore the cave."

"That's another thing. Will you call Eddie for me? Make him promise—swear—he won't go without us. I'm going to visit Mama. We can go day after tomorrow."

"Okay. Anything wrong? I thought you always visited on Sunday."

"No, Dad's just in the mood. I'll call when I get back." Marc hung up, walked back through the living room without his dad's saying anything, and went to his room.

They set out early the next morning. It was another sunny day. Marc itched to be on his bike, heading for the cave. Then he felt guilty for the thought. Mama was going to be happy to see them before Sunday. Bluedog and Marc sat and looked out the window, and he tried to forget the cave.

Mama squealed when she saw them, and a big smile came over her face. It was worth postponing exploring the cave. Marc ran to hug her. Every time he saw her, she looked smaller. She had been sitting on the porch at the sanatorium with her back to the sun, rocking as if that was all the day held for her. She didn't even have the knitting she usually had in her lap.

"My lands, Marc. You're growing so fast!" She tousled his hair and patted Bluedog, who wiggled all over at her touch.

"Hi, Mama. Surprised to see us?" Marc asked, as he and Bluedog sat on the steps at her feet.

"I sure am. Norman, why didn't you tell me you were coming early this week?" She turned her cheek up for his father's kiss.

Visiting Mama was the only time Marc's dad looked and acted normal. He smiled. "Then it wouldn't have been a surprise."

"Shouldn't you be working?" she asked, half scolding.

"The work will wait. I've got clients coming out of my ears. They'll call or come back, and I'll work all day Saturday."

Saturday was usually a half workday. His father stayed open for the farmers and people who couldn't get in during the week. Marc listened to his dad lie to his mother. But Marc would never tell her the truth himself. He didn't want to worry her.

"What are you doing now that school is out, Marc?" Mama asked, taking her son's hand in hers. Even her hands were tiny. Marc's hand looked like a man's hand in hers.

"Oh, not much. Riding my bike, messing around with Hermie and Eddie. They miss you, too. Mrs. Harrington doesn't like us in her kitchen, and even Gramma Sparks's cookies don't hold up to yours. There's a reward out for anyone finding Indian relics. We may poke around a bit, look for a grave everyone has missed."

"Well, if anyone can find it, you can, Marc. I wish I could be out there with you in the woods." Mama looked like a little girl, the way she'd taken to wearing her blond hair in braids since she'd come to Boonville. Easy to care for, she'd said, when his dad asked her why.

She looked tired every time they came, though, and her skin had gotten so pale. Marc had promised her he wouldn't worry about her, but it was hard to keep that promise. What he could do was not let her know he worried.

"I'll go say hi to Mr. Clearwater," Marc said, after they had visited for a while. They never stayed too long, and Marc knew his parents needed a little time to themselves. "Stay here, Bluedog. Be a good girl." He watched until she curled up under the steps.

Roy Clearwater was a full-blooded Osage. On good days he could remember some things about his childhood, or he'd tell Marc legends about the Osage Indian tribes, and how they came to settle in Arkansas. He said if he had any living relatives they were in Oklahoma now, on the reservation there, but his stories were about the past. The Osage had lived north of the Arkansas River and were a very warlike tribe. They had come into the area hunting buffalo and stayed because there were plenty of game animals. Marc figured any arrowheads he found in the woods were Osage, and most relics he and his dad had were from the Osage tribes.

When the Cherokee moved into their territory, there was nothing but trouble. Fort Smith was established to help keep the peace. Mr. Clearwater still got angry when he talked about the Cherokee. The old Indian man was a good story-teller; Marc could imagine the fierce battles between the warring tribes.

"Hello, Mr. Clearwater," Marc said. His friend was sitting by the window looking out, probably visiting the past. "You look healthy enough to do a rain dance, but please don't. I've had enough rain for the whole summer."

Roy Clearwater chuckled. His eyes were clear. It was one of his good days. Most of the patients at the sanatorium were very thin, but he had somehow escaped losing weight. He was very tall. He had wattles under his chin like a turkey, and his face was lined and dark like old leather. He had a high forehead and wore his hair, still only peppered with gray, combed back and down his shoulders. With a little imagination, Marc could see him in full headdress and one of those fringed leather outfits with lots of beadwork on the shirt—or maybe with a robe wrapped around his shoulders. Roy Clearwater had a picture of himself as a boy, but he had on an ordinary shirt and wore a plain rawhide headband. Had Marc seen too many movies? Did real Indians dress a lot plainer than they did on the screen?

Marc couldn't think about anything but the cave. "Did

you ever go into any caves when you were a boy, Mr. Clearwater?" He knew that very early dwellers in Arkansas lived in the bluffs and maybe in some caves. The Osage were probably kin to those people.

"Oh yes. I used to look for things. Spears and . . ." The old man's voice drifted off. He was back in the past.

Marc waited patiently, but Mr. Clearwater began to hum. The tune was almost a chant. From past experience Marc knew when he did that, he would stay wherever he had retreated for longer than Marc had to visit. He got up and said good-bye. Mr. Clearwater didn't hear it. He might not even remember Marc had been there. It made Marc sad, but maybe it was easier for him to live in the past. It had to be more interesting than the sanatorium.

Marc liked the old Indian man. And Mr. Clearwater seemed to like Marc. He told Marc once that his wife and son had died a long time ago. So he had no close kin. Marc teased him that he'd be his kinfolk if he'd let Marc be Osage.

Maybe he'd tell Mr. Clearwater what he and Hermie and Eddie found in the cave. Mr. Clearwater would never tell anyone, or if he did, they would think he was talking about days gone by. Their secret would be safe.

Marc's dad was extra quiet on the way home. Finally Marc broke the stillness. "Is Mama ever going to get well?"

"Of course she is, boy. It's only a matter of time." His father seemed angry that Marc had asked such a thing. But Marc wanted to know. He didn't want someone to lie to him or to tell him half-truths—or call him boy, for that matter. He had a name. Had his father forgotten it?

Usually they ate lunch at the sanatorium with Mama, but today they had left early and gotten home just after one o'clock. Marc got his own lunch. Marc wondered if his father was going to eat anything, but he didn't ask. If his dad wanted to ignore food or his son or anything else, Marc would try to ignore him, too. Especially now that he had a reason to sneak away from home quietly.

He piled a slice of bread with bologna, swiss cheese, lettuce, tomato, and another slice of bologna for good measure. Then he spread mayonnaise on the top piece of bread, turned the sandwich over, and smeared mustard on the other slice. It was a real Dagwood Bumstead creation. He could hardly get it into his mouth to take a bite. Bluedog sat nearby hoping he'd drop half of it. He had gone out on the back step to eat. He liked being outside, and he didn't want to be in the house with his dad right then.

After topping off the sandwich with two glasses of milk and four cookies, Marc called Hermie.

"I'm back already, Hermie. We might have time to look around in the cave if we hurry."

"I forgot I had to go to the dentist today, Marc. Mom is waving at me to hurry right now. She's taking an hour off from work."

"You'll do anything to get out of going into the cave, won't you, Hermie? This is going to be the adventure of a lifetime—or at least of the summer."

"That's what I'm afraid of. You and Eddie go on without me. I'll be disappointed, but I'll try to get over it."

"I don't want to go without you, Hermie. We'll wait until tomorrow, as planned. Eight o'clock, with sack lunches and warm clothes. Promise? You won't invent another excuse? A haircut? A date with Louanne Swartzberger?"

Louanne Swartzberger was a girl in their class who was twice the size of Hermie and still growing, both up and out. She had chosen Hermie for a partner the day they had folk dance lessons in gym. Hermie suddenly had the worst appendicitis attack anyone in fifth grade had ever seen. Eddie and Marc secretly presented Hermie with an Academy Award for his performance, it had worked so well. Louanne was so mad she didn't speak to Hermie the rest of the year.

"I'll think about it while the dentist fills my tooth. I might decide the cave is the worse of two evils."

Marc laughed and hung up. Then he thought of calling Eddie or going to the cave alone. But no one ever went spelunking without a partner. It just wasn't safe; anything could happen. He'd have to wait. At least he didn't have to worry about hurrying. The cave had remained hidden for years; no one else was going to find it by tomorrow.

"Bluedog," Marc called. She had given up on the sandwich and flopped in the shade of the huge oak tree in back of their house. "Want to go swimming?"

Bluedog's tail turned into a flag waving a Fourth of July salute. "Go" was her favorite word, and she loved water. She was ready.

The swimming hole down by the river where kids hung out all summer would be jammed, but it would give Marc something to do. He knew he couldn't just wait or even sit still enough to read. He was too excited about what the morning might bring.

8

THE CAVE'S SECRET

The next day Marc pretended to be asleep until he knew his father had eaten breakfast and gone into his office. Then he scrambled out of bed and hurried to gather up his spelunking gear. Dad had put his personal stuff in the shed behind their house. On the way out Marc got his dad's helmet and carbide lamp for Hermie. He had told Hermie to wear his oldest clothes and shoes. The cave might be muddy.

Bluedog wanted to go. Marc debated, knowing it was foolish to take a dog on a caving expedition. If there was some climbing, even scrambling up and over rocks, Bluedog would be a nuisance. On the other hand, Marc made a habit of taking her everywhere except to school. He'd be gone all day. And she *had* discovered the cave. He could make her sit and stay if they got into territory too difficult for her. Fortunately she was very well behaved. *Probably better behaved than I am,* Marc thought with a smile. He felt guilty going off without telling his father where he would be, but he knew he could never stand it if his dad said he couldn't go.

He ate a bowl of cereal while he thought about taking the dog. By the time he tipped up the bowl and drained the rest of the milk, he had voted yes. Bluedog, the spelunking dog. He hoped he wouldn't regret the decision. To his gear he added an old T-shirt for lowering her into the cave. It was still amazing to him that she had fallen into it while chasing the rabbit without getting hurt. She must have slid most of the way. And maybe her jumping ability had taught her to land safely. Yep, she'd be okay in the cave.

Marc took the precaution of hiding all their gear in his backpack and a duffel bag. If they ran into Mooney again, their supplies wouldn't give away where they were going. He'd say they were going to camp out.

"Hi, Hermie." Marc met Hermie at his back door. "Ready?"

"I guess so." Hermie sounded resigned to his fate. He was eating a banana and had a lunch sack big enough for two days' worth of food.

"Planning on staying underground overnight?" Marc asked, pointing to his sack and laughing.

"Lordy, I hope not. But I might get hungry. Where's Eddie?"

"He said he'd meet us here." Hermie and Marc sat on the back steps of Hermie's house and waited. A half hour went by. Marc started to wiggle as much as Bluedog, who kept staring at him and smiling. *Why aren't we going someplace?* she was asking.

Eddie slid his bike to a stop in the driveway. "Sorry I'm late. Gramma made me go to the store for her." He popped a comb out of his pocket and slipped it through both sides of his hair, as if riding over to Hermie's had put it out of place. No way, with the Brylcream plastering it down.

"Think you'll meet Louanne in the cave?" Hermie often gave Eddie a bad time about having his hair so neat. Eddie just threw Hermie a dirty look and put his comb away.

"I thought you might have had trouble slipping away." Marc saw that Eddie had his gear hidden in an old backpack, too.

"Nah. Pops was dozing on the front porch. No one cares where I am."

No one cares where I am either, Marc thought. Then he remembered to be glad about that, this time.

"Okay, let's go." Marc slipped on his pack and called to Bluedog, who was napping under the steps.

"Holy Cow! You taking that dog?" Eddie asked, with disbelief.

"Sure. She found the cave. She deserves to go."

"That's dumb, Marc. A dog in a cave? That's a bunch of horse pucky." Eddie pulled out and rode ahead of Marc and Hermie. It might be, Marc admitted again to himself, but he was determined to try Bluedog in the cave. She looked up at him and smiled as he got on his bike. "You want to go, don't you, Bluedog, don't you girl?"

She barked and bounced, eager to run.

Their luck held, and they didn't run into Mooney or anyone else who might ask where they were going. They did take the precaution, though, of hiding their bikes at the cutoff and looking in all directions before they disappeared into the brush and headed toward the cave entrance.

Bluedog didn't want to go back into the hole, but Marc went first and had Eddie and Hermie lower her down. She whined and leaned against Marc's legs when he took her out of the sling. "Good girl, Blue, good girl." He reassured the dog that he would be with her.

"I don't like this," Hermie said, when he tumbled in a

heap beside Marc, knocking his glasses off. He had walked his way down the slope like Marc had instructed, but he let go of the rope before he got his footing.

"Everyone is scared at first," Marc told him. "It's normal. Even some good cavers admit to being claustrophobic in tight spots."

"We're not in a tight spot and I'm already feeling it," said Hermie, looking glum.

"I was never afraid." Eddie swung over beside them and untied the rope from his waist. They left it dangling there, tied to the rock above. They had used Eddie's rope.

"I'm going to leave my rope here," Marc decided. He laid the heavy coil up against the wall of the cave where they had come down. "If we have to climb where we need a rope, I'll come back and get it, or we'll do the climb another day. I don't want to carry that weight all over."

Marc had shown Hermie how to light his dad's carbide lamp while they were in daylight, waiting for Eddie. Marc had cleaned both lamps after his swimming trip the day before. There was a satisfying *pop* as his lamp flared and burned brightly.

"What if our lights burn out before we get back?" asked Hermie.

Just the idea of being caught in any cave without light made Marc's stomach do flip-flops. "Don't worry, Hermie, I always carry a flashlight and a supply of candles. My matches are in an old Band-Aid can to keep them dry."

"I feel like a miner," said Hermie, buckling on the helmet Marc had handed him after taping his lamp to the front.

"As much as I like exploring underground," Marc said, "working in a mine would be the last job I'd choose."

It took about twenty-five steps to lose the small amount of light coming from the entrance. "I don't like this," Hermie said again. His voice sounded funny bouncing off the rock walls.

Their lights cast huge shadows around them. The passageway narrowed down, and there was a drop-off on the right.

"Where does that go?" Hermie asked, peering downward.

"I don't think it goes anywhere." Marc shined his light into it. "For my money, it's just a hole."

"We could walk right into a hole like that," said Hermie.

"Stay with us," Eddie said, "and watch for holes."

A shiver flew up Marc's back. He didn't want to tell Hermie that he was both scared and excited every time he entered a cave. If Hermie thought Marc was the least bit scared, he'd turn back.

"Look at those big rocks just sitting up there." Hermie pointed his light overhead. "Any of them could fall on us. I don't like that idea at all."

"Hermie, would you stop worrying!" Eddie was disgusted.

"Well they could, couldn't they, Marc? I read about that Floyd Collins guy who was trapped in a cave by a falling rock. And he was an experienced caver."

"You read too much," said Eddie. "If you're going to whine the whole time we're in here, go back and wait for us."

"Alone?" asked Hermie. He stopped worrying out loud, but one glance at his face told Marc he was really scared.

"I still think it was stupid to bring Bluedog," Eddie said, and took off in the lead. He stopped to scramble into the drop-off and confirm that it went nowhere. "How can she climb anything?"

"She's my dog." Marc was more tired of Eddie's remarks than of Hermie's being scared. "I'll be responsible for her. She might even find something we'd miss."

"Dogs have a great sense of smell." Hermie stated the obvious, probably just to change the subject from caves.

Eddie twisted his remark. "Yeah, especially when they're wet." He laughed and hurried on. Marc let him go. He planned to stay with Hermie and help him get over being afraid.

"Think we'll find gold?" Hermie was still thinking about mining, or trying to cheer himself up.

"Something better," Marc predicted. "I hope we'll find evidence of Indians. I'll bet the Osage knew every cave in this area. Sometimes they used them for storage or for hiding things."

Bluedog was acting strange. She didn't run ahead or back and forth like she did when they were in the woods. In fact, she stayed so close to Marc that he had trouble walking.

"I think Bluedog's scared, too," Marc told Hermie and laughed.

"Smart dog." Hermie walked almost as close as Bluedog. Marc felt like a human magnet.

The cave was cold and damp. Marc shivered, even wearing his sweatshirt and denim jacket. Most caves are around fifty-five degrees inside, quite a change from the summer ninety-degree temperatures above ground. Marc knew he'd get used to the cold soon. He was probably sweaty from riding his bike.

They had walked about a city block when they came to Eddie, who was stopped before them. He had squatted down and was nibbling on a Baby Ruth bar.

"Jumpin' Jehoshaphat!" said Hermie. They shined their lights on the wall. Sheets of water had formed rippled and folded flowstone. A couple of stalactites had come all the way down to meet stalagmites on the floor, forming slender columns.

"Not bad," said Eddie, "but I've seen better. Which way do you want to go?" One pathway headed downhill, another continued straight ahead.

"You choose, Hermie," Marc suggested. "We'll stay together."

"How will we know how to get back to the opening, if we wander around in here?" Hermie wanted to be sure they got out.

"I'm making a map." Eddie showed Hermie a scrap of paper and a stub of pencil he carried in his pocket. He had made a Y and sketched in the two columns and the flowstone. "You need to remember to turn and look back occasionally, too. Things look different from the other side."

Marc had a good sense of direction. He hardly ever bothered writing anything down. But he did take careful note of everything he saw on the walls, weird rocks, bumps along the path, formations.

"That way." Hermie pointed straight ahead. "It's bigger."

"Might be a pretty good cave," Eddie said, before they went the way Hermie had chosen.

"I can hear water dripping," Marc said. "At least it's a live cave."

"Are there dead caves?" Hermie asked, a funny hitch in his voice.

Marc laughed. "A dead cave is dry. Live caves have water dripping or running into them, and formations are still growing."

"I got a book and read it after going to the dentist yesterday," Hermie said. "I thought there'd be more stalactites and stalagmites. And some crystals and those neat soda straw things."

"They only put the best caves in books, Hermie." Eddie stuffed his candy wrapper back into his pack. "You probably won't see all that fancy stuff down here. That flowstone may be the best formation in here."

The cave had more piled rock than Marc had ever seen. There were loads of huge boulders stacked on each other.

The path Hermie had chosen came to a dead end almost immediately. There wasn't even the promise of a crawl space. The ceiling lowered. Eddie got down and waddled to the end of the passageway.

"Nothing," he reported when he wiggled out.

They retraced their steps and took the other tunnel. Soon it slid steeply downhill, narrowed, and the ceiling lowered again.

"Horse pucky," Eddie complained. "Two paths leading to zero."

"Then we have to go back home," said Hermie, his voice hopeful.

"Let's be sure." Marc shined his light up and down both walls while Eddie belly flopped and scrambled into the end of the tunnel they were in.

Eddie never hesitated to crawl into the narrow spaces. Marc envied his daring; he was always nervous when he had to crawl into or through a tight spot. He'd been spelunking long enough to know he probably would never get over that tiny fear. So he forced himself to push it back and keep going. He trusted his dad, though, and that helped. Now he was with Hermie, who had never been caving before, and Eddie, who seemed to have no fear. From other times they'd gone together, Marc knew Eddie was sometimes reckless. He felt it paid to be cautious underground.

"Look, Marc! Up there." Eddie pointed to a spot near the ceiling of the cave. "Boost me up. I think there's an opening behind that huge boulder."

Marc's heart pounded. He could see what Eddie had spotted. He shined his light and examined the ledge, but he couldn't tell from the ground if it was a tunnel. Giving Eddie a leg up, he watched him grab hold of an outcropping of rock, pull himself level, then disappear. His legs dangled for a couple of seconds, sneakers scraping the hole, sending pebbles down the wall. The rocks bounced and echoed through the underground passageway.

"That's a creepy sound." Hermie sat down to dig in his pack. He pulled out half a bologna sandwich to give him strength. "I don't like this."

"You already said that." Marc laughed and sat beside him. "Three times."

"I'll probably say it again—in fact, right now. I still don't like this." Hermie bit into the sandwich. It was so quiet Marc could hear Hermie chewing.

"This is more like it." Eddie's head appeared above them. "There's a big room over here, and tunnels go off in all directions. One heads downhill."

"You guys go on," Hermie decided, giving Bluedog the rest of his sandwich. "I'll wait here with Bluedog. She can't get up there."

"I've been thinking about that," Marc said. "I figure I can lift her up. One of you can pull her through the hole. She may not like it, but she can do it. Stretched out, she's skinnier than any of us. You go on up, Hermie. Then lean down and take Blue's forefeet. I'll boost her up."

Hermie grumbled. "If I get stuck, you guys will be sorry."

"Yes we will, so don't. I'll never get out of here." Eddie reached for Hermie's hand to help him onto the ledge.

Marc almost fell trying to boost Hermie up. Then, when Marc pushed on his rear, Hermie lost his balance and fell back, nearly squashing Marc. "Come on, Hermie. I can't lift you. You have to help. Grab a knob of rock or something."

Groaning, Eddie pulled and Marc pushed. "Holy Cow, Hermie," Eddie complained. "You've got to lose some weight if we're going to do this all summer."

"I'm not going to do this all summer." Hermie bellied over the ledge and into the hole.

It couldn't be any harder to get Bluedog through. Except

that she didn't want to go. She whimpered and licked Marc's face as if to say, *"Do I have to?"*

"Come on, Bluedog. You can do it." Marc lifted her, leaning against the wall. Bluedog's hind legs pushed on his chest and kicked him in the chin, but Eddie managed to lean over far enough to get a good hold. He pulled her through the hole.

"I can't believe I'm spelunking with a dog," Eddie said, as he leaned back through the hole and reached for Marc. "Hold my legs," he called back to Hermie, who had wiggled through the short crawl. "Hey, I'm glad you went on through. If you'd have gotten stuck, we'd be on this side. We could go home."

"And leave me here, stuck, I guess. That's not funny, Eddie."

Eddie laughed anyway. Being taller than Hermie, Marc managed to jump and grab Eddie's outstretched hands. Hermie held onto Eddie so Marc wouldn't pull him off the ledge. Eddie wiggled backwards, into the hole, and Marc braced his feet on the wall until he could grab a rock in the opening. Then he pulled himself up onto the ledge and slid through the hole. There was a pile of dirt on the other side, so it was easy to slide down. Getting back through would be a cinch.

Bluedog danced and barked when Marc slid down beside her. Her voice echoed, sounding strange in the hollow underground tunnels. Marc laughed. "I've never heard a dog barking in a cave. Good dog, Blue, good girl."

"Gee." Hermie looked around as far as he could see with his headlamp. "This room is as big as the school cafeteria."

"Almost. I'm going to check for tunnels off to the right." Eddie went on, not waiting for Hermie and Marc.

"We'll go the other way and meet you," Marc called to Eddie. Marc's stomach felt as if it were full of bats, wings whirring against his insides. He was certain they were going to find something neat. The cave itself was thrilling, but he wanted more.

"Here's a tunnel," Hermie said with excitement in his voice. Marc hoped he was starting to forget his fear and see how much fun exploring a cave could be.

"We won't go in until we see what Eddie found." Marc led the way around the big room.

"Hey, look up here," Hermie said pointing. "There's a crack along the middle of the ceiling. All those rocks up there look like dinosaur bones."

They did. The spine of a brontosaurus. It was probably just a coincidence, but stranger burial grounds for dinosaurs had been found. Marc didn't think there had been any dinosaurs found in Arkansas.

"There are two tunnels over here, and one of them branches off." Eddie reported when they caught up to him. "I've got an idea. Let's split up—each of us take a tunnel. We walk for five minutes or until it pinches down, then come back here, ten minutes in all. That'll save time and give us an idea of the length of each tunnel."

"I don't want to go off by myself." Hermie's voice wavered.

"Look, it's just upright walking. If you have to crawl, you turn around and come back." Eddie had no patience with Hermie's fear.

"Walk straight, Hermie. Don't make any turn-offs to other tunnels. Map it in your mind, though. Walk straight in, straight out." Marc thought Eddie had a good idea. And it was safe enough. "Okay, look at your watches." Marc shined his light on his wrist.

"You take the first one I passed, Hermie," Eddie suggested. "It was big and wide. Not even you could get stuck.

It's probably the main tunnel. Go around those big rocks."

"Okay, Hermie?" Marc asked, giving his friend a chance to back out.

"Okay," Hermie agreed reluctantly. "Five minutes."

"I'll go back over to the other end," Marc said to Eddie. "You take this one. Don't do anything crazy, Eddie."

"I won't." Eddie sounded disgusted. But Marc knew Eddie. He could get carried away, and if one of them got into trouble, they'd all be in trouble.

Marc patted Bluedog and snapped his fingers, telling her to follow him. Bluedog had relaxed a little and trotted right beside Marc as he hurried back to his tunnel.

To his disappointment, the pathway didn't last long. It ended in a mound of flowstone—at least it was pretty. Marc shined his light so he could see the formation better. It looked like the hind end of an elephant, complete with narrow tail. It was orangy and slick where iron water had run over it for centuries. As he turned around, starting back, Bluedog began to whine.

"What's wrong, Blue? What's the matter, girl?" Marc leaned down and patted her. Then he shined his light in the direction she was looking.

The tunnel didn't stop after all, but turned an abrupt corner beside the elephant. Marc looked at his watch. He'd been gone five minutes. He shined his light around. This was the only opening. He'd follow it a few steps.

Bluedog didn't want to go with him. After they squeezed by the flowstone, she sat down and continued to stare into the darkness. A chill crept up the back of Marc's neck. He could feel those little hairs there standing up as stiff as a scrub brush. What could Bluedog see that he couldn't? What could be in there—an animal?

Marc didn't think there'd be any animal in the cave unless it was a bat. Would Bluedog be afraid of a bat?

"Come on, Blue. You're being silly. I'll go first."

Slowly Marc made his way into the smaller tunnel. His helmet scraped the top of the passageway. He stooped over, took one step, looked all around. One step, a look around. He could almost feel his ears stretching for any sound. It seemed quieter than usual, if that was possible.

He and his dad had split up occasionally when it seemed safe, but right now Marc was terribly aware that he was all alone. He'd never had such a creepy feeling. Bluedog had made him feel this way. He glanced back. She sat watching Marc, not even smiling.

"Come on, Blue." She brushed her tail on the floor. But she sat there like she had plopped down in Elmer's glue.

"Silly dog," Marc said loudly. He took a deep breath and turned around.

Another step, another look. Another step, another look. About ten steps into the passageway, Marc could see far enough ahead to realize the tunnel ended. All this getting scared for nothing. He relaxed, lowering his lamp to study the floor. Then something at the end of the narrow corridor caught his eye. It was a long, rounded heap of dirt—not a natural formation.

And at the far end, pushed neatly into the mound, was the shaft of an arrow.

9

PLANS RUINED

Jumpin' Jehoshaphat! It was a grave! An Indian grave!

For a minute Marc stood there, staring at the grave. Then he looked closer at the arrow without touching it. The grave wasn't big, not nearly big enough for an adult. In fact . . . He paced it off. Most Indians were shorter than people today. It might be someone about his age, he thought, and wished he hadn't.

He glanced at his watch. He'd been gone twenty minutes. He was overdue, and he didn't want Hermie and Eddie to worry. He knew he had to go back immediately.

"Come on, Bluedog. It was dumb to be afraid of a grave." But in a way, Blue had told Marc that something out of the ordinary was in the side tunnel. Thank goodness he had followed it, and that she had sensed something, whatever it was.

"Where've you been?" Hermie was worried.

"You went farther. That's not fair." Eddie stood up. "We agreed on ten minutes, long enough to see if any tunnel was good enough to explore later."

"Mine stopped," Hermie said, before Marc could explain why he'd run over the time limit. "There was just a big pile of dirt."

"A breakdown," Eddie said. "That's called a breakdown. Maybe there was a passageway once, but rocks and dirt slid into it. My tunnel goes on and on. I've sat here long enough—let's explore it."

"Doesn't anyone want to know what I found?" Marc smiled. He was going to bowl them over.

"Yeah, what?" Eddie didn't think Marc could top his long passageway.

"A grave."

"A grave!" they shouted together.

"Holy Cow! Whose?" Eddie was finally impressed.

"It must be Indian. There's an arrow at the head. Probably Osage, probably pretty old."

"Let's go see!" Eddie practically ran across the big room toward Marc's tunnel.

Bluedog barked, hearing the excitement in Eddie's voice.

"Bluedog wouldn't go in there," Marc told them as he caught up with Eddie and led the way past the elephant to the grave site. "That scared me."

"Maybe she saw a ghost," said Hermie.

Marc laughed. "Yeah, maybe so."

They all stood looking at the small grave. Finally Hermie let out a long, low whistle. "A real grave. Should we dig it up?"

"Sure. But we don't have the tools to do it today," Marc said. "Besides, it's getting late. If I'm not back for supper Dad will remember to wonder where I've been all day. He'll ask questions for sure. And anyway, it'll take a long time to dig this up right."

Hermie looked at his watch. "Hey, I forgot to get hungry. And I have to be home for supper, too."

"The reward poster said to just find a grave. We can save

the work of digging it up by telling Professor Beslow to come in here and dig it up himself." Eddie wasn't one to work hard unless he had to.

"Wait a minute, Eddie. I want to see what's in it before we tell anyone, don't you?" Marc asked. "I want the fun of digging it up. There might be nothing but a skeleton and this arrow. . . ."

Yet Marc had a feeling there was more. A person's belongings were usually buried with him, along with things to keep him happy on the way to the other side. He'd be surprised if there weren't any more relics.

"But then again, if there's some good stuff, we can decide what to do about it," Marc finished his argument.

"You just want to keep it for yourself," Eddie said.

"That wouldn't be fair. It doesn't belong to me."

"You found it," said Hermie. "You could keep it and no one but us would know."

"You're right, but that's not fair. All of us agreed on sharing the reward." Eddie wasn't going to forget about the money.

"Look, let's go home. It will take us a little time to get out of here. I don't want my dad asking questions or telling me I can't come back."

"We can come back tomorrow with a shovel." Hermie had forgotten he was afraid of being underground.

"Small garden spades, a toothbrush, a box, and some tissue paper." Marc started to list the things they'd need. "We'll have to dig carefully."

Bluedog started to bark again. She'd barked enough today for a whole month. But she sensed their excitement. She had walked right up to the grave this time.

"I guess she wants to come again." Hermie petted her.

"She found the cave. She found the grave. I don't think I'd have noticed the opening behind the flowstone," Marc admitted. "It's fairly well hidden."

"A dog for a partner." Eddie sighed and started out. "Holy Cow, who'd have thought it?"

"Don't let Eddie give you a bad time, Blue," Hermie told the dog. "You're a good finder, and we need you on our team."

It was three days before they got to go back into the cave. Hermie had another dental appointment, then his mother made him go shopping with her. Marc's dad wanted to go back to the sanatorium on Sunday, and Marc could hardly say he had something more exciting to do. He felt ashamed. It was the first time he had not really wanted to go and visit Mama. He thought she'd understand, though, if he could tell her. He hoped Eddie wouldn't go alone. It would be just like him to do that.

Maybe he wasn't as brave as he acted, though, because he waited for them. On Monday they got their gear together at Hermie's place. Marc had taken the back streets, Bluedog trotting along beside him. It was getting hotter by the day, coming around to what June was supposed to be like. That cave was going to feel good.

All the great things they might find raced through his head. But he kept remembering Mooney's plan to let them find something, then somehow claim it for himself.

The three of them rode their bikes in a row at a leisurely pace, as if they had no plan for the day. Only their loaded packs suggested the adventure ahead. Somehow Marc wasn't surprised, though, when Mooney and Otis Kruger showed up in front of them at the last street crossing before the old highway. Of all the dumb luck. Marc was getting tired of Mooney's antics.

Marc stopped, leaned his bike over, and took hold of Bluedog's collar. She had started to growl the minute Mooney showed his face.

"I never saw a dog who was a better judge of character."

Eddie stopped beside Marc. Bluedog had lowered her head and arched her back. Marc thought she'd have pounced on Mooney if he hadn't held onto her. He didn't know why she acted that way toward him, unless she sensed that Marc didn't like him.

"Going on a picnic?" asked Mooney, ignoring Eddie's remark and Bluedog's growling.

"Maybe," Hermie answered. "The wildflowers are beautiful in the woods, Mooney. We thought we'd gather some for your funeral. After Bluedog chews you up, that is."

"Very funny, Hermie. Don't you think so, Otis? This kid is very funny. He could try out for the Colgate Comedy Hour on TV and come out with first place, easy."

"Sure, Mooney. He's real funny." Otis repeated Mooney's words. His lip curled up into a smile.

"I think we'll go along for the ride." Mooney backed up his bike and made a sweeping bow, suggesting that Marc and his friends could continue their journey courtesy of his generosity.

What could they do? Maybe Marc should've turned Bluedog loose, but he didn't want her poisoned from biting Mooney. He led the way down the road, insisting that Bluedog come with him. They rode leisurely out the highway toward the cave, but when they reached the turn-off, Mooney and Otis still followed. So Marc kept going.

About a mile past the bluffs was a small picnic area. A wide pull-off from the highway overlooked the river with mountains in the distance. Mostly tourists stopped there. The scenery around Pine Creek didn't seem spectacular if you'd seen it almost every day of your life.

"Any ideas?" Marc said in a low voice when they were all seated at a picnic table.

Mooney and Otis sat on their bikes at the edge of the road and grinned. Mooney pulled a weed stem and chewed on it.

They knew they'd interrupted something. Obviously, riding out to picnic at the overlook at nine o'clock in the morning wasn't Marc and his friends' usual activity.

"This is a bunch of horse pucky," Eddie said. "We haven't a prayer of shaking them. Mooney is too suspicious."

"They know we're going someplace with these loaded packs." Hermie looked inside his canvas backpack and pulled out a banana. "Might as well enjoy our rest stop."

Marc shook his head, frustrated. He liked his plans to run smoothly. He stared out over the valley with the river in the distance. It was so clear this morning he could imagine he could see the walleye in the river.

"We could go fishing," he said to keep the conversation going. "Wait, I do have an idea. We don't give a hoot if it's night or day when we're in the cave. It's dark in there all the time. We'll go tonight." Marc lowered his voice to a whisper. "I'll say I'm spending the night with Hermie."

"And I'll say I'm spending the night with you." Hermie caught on immediately.

"Why don't both of you say you're spending the night with me?" suggested Eddie. "Pops and Gramma go to bed at dark and neither of them hears very well. We could start from my house, and no one would ever know we'd left."

"Let's go back and get our suits and go swimming, then. We can lie around all day. Mooney and Otis will surely get tired of watching us after a while." Marc led the way to the bikes, trying to keep from laughing. Boy howdy, they'd outsmart Mooney yet.

"Get your bat, Marc," Eddie added before they took off. "We'll hit some flies and grounders till noon. Then the water will feel really good."

"I'll bring my new Super Man and Plastic Man comics," Hermie said.

"Got any to trade?" Eddie asked.

"Not yet." Hermie puffed to keep up.

As if it had been their plan all along, they rode back to town, split up, got their suits on, and met back at the river road east of town. They acted as if Mooney and Otis had spoiled nothing for them.

To their surprise Mooney and Otis followed them to the river. But as Mooney sat skipping rocks in the shallow water upstream from the swimming hole, Marc knew he was getting bored.

It was a long day. Marc got bored, too. Hermie and Eddie dozed on the old blanket that Hermie brought from home. By then they'd played ball, gone swimming, eaten lunch, read all the comics they'd brought, talked the night's plan to death, then run out of things to do.

Marc wished he could sleep. But his mind was turning cartwheels. He kept dreaming of the possibilities that the grave might hold. They had that fifty dollars cinched. And his father would be amazed he'd made such a discovery on his own.

10

NIGHT ADVENTURE

Dinner was different only because his dad brought home a lot of groceries. Marc dug in the bags. Fritos, a can of peanuts, and strawberry ice cream. Boy howdy, they'd eat at last. Marc didn't ask his dad where he'd been, whether he'd sold a policy, what possessed him to go to the store—anything about his day.

"Is it all right if I spend the night at Eddie's?" Marc got up his nerve to ask. He couldn't think of any reason for his father to mess up their plans, but then he'd been unpredictable all year.

"I don't want you boys hanging around downtown."

"Don't worry about that, we don't like hanging out downtown. And we've seen the movie, three times. We practically have it memorized."

"Why don't you ask Mr. Daniels whether he has some jobs you could do this summer?"

That was the most Marc's dad had said to him in a long time, the most interest he'd shown in his son's activities or whereabouts since January. Part of Marc was glad; part of him wanted his father to keep ignoring him, at least until after they'd explored the cave.

"That's a great idea, Dad. I'll ride over tomorrow and ask." Marc didn't know why he hadn't thought of it. He reached for another slice of fried Spam and piled his plate with corn niblets. It was a super idea. He'd like it much better than Mooney's paper route.

When dinner was over, his dad took his coffee into the living room and turned on the television, as usual. Marc knew he could leave any time without his knowing or caring—well, as soon as he'd done the dishes. He squeezed Ivory liquid into the dishpan and waited while the hot water made it foam into a pile of suds.

Everything was greasy, but he made fast work of it, even the skillet. Piling dishes into the drainer to dry, he looked in the freezer to see what else his dad had bought. Fudgesickles! Boy howdy, he must've sold a policy.

Marc had left his pack loaded with stuff from the morning, except for his lunch, which he'd taken to the swimming hole. Now he threw an apple and a peach into a bag and stuck it inside the top flap. They'd be home for breakfast.

"Let's try again, Bluedog." Marc motioned for her to come with him. She smiled and was glad to trot along. She had slept all afternoon after a dip in the river.

They slipped away from Eddie's just as dusk was fading into night. The first star appeared. Marc wished on it for good luck in the cave. He had this sure feeling that the grave was going to hold something special for them.

"It's not safe to ride without lights," Hermie pointed out as they got onto the highway. Hermie took spells of being cautious. Marc knew he was right, but hardly anybody drove far in Pine Creek at night.

"What can we do?" Eddie said. "Get out our headlamps and light the way? Stop acting like a sissy, Hermie."

"We can pull over on the shoulder when a car comes," Marc suggested. "There won't be that much traffic."

The night was so quiet they could hear cars approaching. Twice they pulled off on the shoulder and huddled near the trees that lined the highway. *With our luck,* Marc thought, *a policeman will drive by and ask what we're doing out here.*

There was no moon, and it was harder to find the cave entrance than they'd thought. "Let's light our headlamps," Marc suggested.

They sat down and poured water into their carbide lamps. Each popped as it blazed on. The air filled with a gassy smell. They had flashlights as well as their headlamps, but they still couldn't see very well—especially with the thick undergrowth.

"Are you sure we took the right turn off the highway?" grumbled Eddie, when a branch slapped him in the face, making his lamp sputter.

Cicadas punctuated the night air with their buzzing. Twice the boys heard the hoot of an owl, then the soft whispers of wings overhead.

"Some people think hearing an owl hoot is bad luck," said Hermie.

Eddie and Marc ignored his remark. Small animals rattled through the brush at intervals alongside them as they made their way in a line toward what they thought was the entrance. Bluedog was no help, since she kept dashing off to sniff for rabbits. She loved wandering around in the woods in the pitch dark.

Finally Eddie literally stumbled into the rocks that bordered the hole. "Holy Cow, I could've fallen off the bluff with just a few more steps."

"We'd have left you there," Marc teased. "I've had it with delays."

Quickly they lowered themselves and Bluedog into the cave. She wasn't any happier about going down on the rope a second time, but she tolerated the boys' helping her. Maybe she was getting used to it.

Once inside the tunnels they forgot it was night outside, since it was always darker than the blackest night underground. Marc boosted Eddie up to the overhead hole. They followed the same pattern as before, getting Hermie, Bluedog, and Marc into the large room.

Bluedog started to whine the minute they reached the end of the short tunnel that led to the grave. Marc felt icy fingers touch the back of his neck and tickle down his spine again.

"Stop that, Bluedog," Eddie said. "You give me the creeps."

"What do you think she sees?" Hermie asked. His voice quivered.

"The Thing." Eddie curled his fingers towards Hermie, reminding them of the scariest movie they'd seen in their whole lives.

"Stop it, Eddie," Hermie demanded. "You're a pile of horse pucky."

"Bluedog can't see any better than you or me in here," Marc said. "She senses something." Marc did too, but he didn't say so. He was afraid Hermie would want to go back, and he was going to stick it out. It was probably just the idea of a grave. They were being silly.

Still, Marc couldn't get past the feeling that someone was watching them or was in there with them. Rubbing both arms to chase away the chill, he chalked it up to an overactive imagination and Bluedog's acting so funny. He had thought so much about what they'd find there that it made him imagine all sorts of things. Like people bringing a body down here to bury it. It certainly didn't get here by itself.

"Why do you think this grave is underground?" he asked, needing to talk.

"Maybe they wanted to hide it. From animals or hostile Indians," suggested Hermie.

"Maybe they believed putting the body in here gave it some kind of supernatural powers," Marc imagined aloud.

"You're giving me the creeps, too, Marc," Eddie said.

"Maybe the Indian died in here. They just buried him where he died," Marc said.

"I wish you hadn't said that," Hermie complained.

Bluedog sat down beside the entrance, by the flowstone, just like she'd done before. When Marc shined his light back at her, she had laid her nose flat on her front paws and prepared to watch, but would come no closer. She whimpered.

"That's the way she acted when I first came in here," Marc said. "You can see why it made me nervous. I know, maybe if this guy was buried here, his ghost couldn't get out. It's trapped down here." Marc joked to stop being scared.

"Marc, stop it, or I'm going back." Hermie moved closer to where Marc stood.

"Alone?" Eddie asked and grinned.

They tried to laugh at Bluedog, and got ready to dig, but Marc still felt uncomfortable. Maybe it was because he'd never dug up a grave before. He'd unearthed a few relics with his father, but even they hadn't found a whole grave. He sure didn't want to think he needed his dad along to do this, though. He took a deep breath and prepared to dig.

All three of them had brought small garden spades, the type used to set in bedding plants. Marc was glad they hadn't had big shovels with them when they were stopped by Mooney and Otis. Then those two would have followed them forever.

Scraping the dry dirt away carefully, they each worked at uncovering the grave. Marc dug at what he assumed from the position of the arrow was the top. Had the arrow belonged to the person who had died, or to the people who had buried him? Had they used it for a marker, or a head-stone?

For a time the only sound in the shadowy darkness was the rasping of metal on dirt.

"Boy howdy, I've found something!" Marc's shovel made a hollow, thudding sound. "Probably a skull." He said it matter-of-factly, but the thought of a grinning skull inside the grave sent shivers over him. Bluedog whined again.

"I'm going to get out of here." Hermie dropped his shovel. He started backing up, then fell over his backpack.

"Go by yourself," Eddie said.

Marc slipped out the paint scraper he had added to his pack at the last minute. Carefully he dug with the edge and scraped away the loose dirt with his fingers. Little by little the skull appeared. The grinning teeth and hollow eyes almost put him off, but he took a deep breath and kept dusting away the powdery dirt.

Hermie squatted on his heels by his pack. Eddie stopped working and watched Marc. He kept scraping, even more carefully.

"I didn't think about how a skeleton was going to look down here," said Hermie.

"What'd you think you were going to find in a grave? Horse pucky?" Eddie started to giggle. They were all glad to laugh.

Eddie and Hermie began to help again. It took a long time to uncover the skeleton and sort through the things buried with the body. As the rib cage came into view, they scraped even more carefully alongside the body. Little by little they lost their fear, and their precaution about digging paid off.

Buried with the boy—they knew it was probably a boy because they found a bow and arrow and girls didn't usually hunt—was a small clay pot. To their surprise there was also the skeleton of an animal in the grave—a small dog, they decided, after looking at the perfect skull.

"Why do you suppose there's a dog buried with him?" Eddie said quietly, as if he were at the funeral.

"Gee, maybe the dog died trying to save his life," Hermie said, imagining the story of the boy's death. "Maybe he drowned in the river, and the dog died trying to pull him out."

"Maybe warriors from a hostile tribe came in and killed him, or caught him and the dog out hunting and killed them both." Eddie made up another story, warming to the game.

"Maybe they had a belief that everything that belonged to the dead person should be buried with him, even if it had to be killed." Hermie picked up the dog's skull and looked it over carefully. "In old India, when a Hindu man died, his wife climbed onto the funeral pyre to die with him—she had to, whether she wanted to or not—and sometimes it's still done!"

"That's a bunch of horse pucky," Eddie said, laying down the toothbrush he'd been scraping with. "You expect me to believe that?"

"I read about it," insisted Hermie.

Marc had no explanation for the Indian boy's death, but seeing the boy lying there beside his dog touched him so that he couldn't speak. He didn't want to. He sat there quietly and listened to Hermie and Eddie making up their stories.

Eddie pushed Hermie aside and lay down beside the skeleton. "Look, he's just about my size. That's creepy."

"Indians were smaller than we are. He might have been our size, but he was probably a few years older," Hermie said. Then they got quiet again.

Marc had never thought much about dying, about turning into a skeleton under a mound of dirt. He'd bet Hermie and Eddie hadn't either. He didn't like thinking about it.

He jumped as something wet touched his hand. Bluedog had edged closer until she sat with them, pushing her nose into Marc's palm. He put his arm around her, and all four of them sat silently. It seemed the right thing to do, to sit there and say nothing, their lights on the grave, shadows dancing off the cave walls.

In the distance they could hear the drip of water. There was no other sound. Bluedog was warm under Marc's arm and made him feel less alone. He shivered, and she licked his face. He laughed, and the spell was broken.

"Well, let's finish uncovering it. There might be arrowheads or small things in here that we haven't found yet." Eddie started brushing dirt away again. "This certainly qualifies for that reward money, don't you think?"

"Yeah," said Hermie softly.

Marc still couldn't say anything. He went back to work, scraping and sifting through the dirt around the skeleton, uncovering the rest of the body and the pot.

When the job was done they'd found a tomahawk, two flint knives, a three-cornered flint spear, and ten perfect, creamy-white arrowheads. A few blue beads showed up. They'd have to sift the dirt to find them all. They arranged it all where they'd uncovered it, so they could see everything in place.

"Hey, it's four in the morning," Marc said, when they had taken the mound down flat, and he looked at his watch.

None of them had noticed the passage of time. They had been so caught up in the digging that they hadn't remembered to be tired or sleepy. They'd forgotten it was the middle of the night.

"We'd better try to get home before Pops and Gramma wake up," said Eddie. "They get up at dawn. It's a habit left over from living on the farm."

"Listen," Marc said, before they got up to trace their steps out of the cave. "Let's leave all our stuff here, leave the grave just like this, and think about what we've found."

"Wait a minute. You mean not tell anyone?" Eddie asked. "Not call Mr. Beslow?"

"Right. Let's have it be our secret for a couple of days. The grave isn't going anywhere. We've got all summer."

"Think what we could do with that money this summer, though." Eddie just couldn't stop thinking about the money. "What if someone else stumbles onto the cave? What if Mooney and Otis search and find it? What if they followed us and we didn't see them?"

"That's almost impossible," Marc reasoned. "And if they had followed us tonight, they'd be right here now. I know you don't understand why I'm asking you to do this. I don't even understand it myself. It's just a feeling I have. A strange feeling—like we've disturbed someone."

"Horse pucky," Eddie said. "We're supposed to back off this find because you feel funny about it? Because we bothered this skeleton? That's stupid." Eddie couldn't believe what Marc was asking him to do.

"Yes, please . . ." Marc practically begged. "If you're my friends, you'll do this."

They sat quietly, everyone thinking. Eddie thought Marc was crazy. Hermie—well, Marc couldn't tell what he thought. And Marc didn't even know why he was asking them to do it.

Finally Hermie said, "Let's humor him, Eddie. We both know he's strange, but what can it hurt?"

"Promise me." Marc stuck out his hand and insisted before Eddie could think about it any longer.

Hermie put his hand in Marc's. Eddie hesitated and scowled, but finally lifted his grimy hand onto theirs. "I must be nuts. Okay—but only for a couple of days."

Brushing off their jeans and jacket sleeves, they hurriedly

got ready to leave. It would take them an hour or so to get out of the cave and get home. The way they looked, someone was sure to ask questions if they saw them. Even Gramma and Pops would realize they hadn't gotten this dirty from just sleeping.

Their luck gave out two blocks from Eddie's house. None of them had remembered about Mooney's paper route. It was six o'clock, and they were thinking about how to crawl into the window of Eddie's room. Eddie said Pops and Gramma never disturbed him, since they knew *he* wasn't going to get up at dawn. All they had to do was get into the room.

"Hey, hey, hey!" Mooney called out as he rode straight in front of them. His bike was heavy with newspapers. He was just starting to deliver. "Now, I know you three are never out this early, because I'm out here every day. Something is going on." He looked them up and down.

Marc followed Mooney's eyes and cursed his carelessness. They were all three filthy from head to foot. There was no way to hide it.

"It doesn't take much intuition to know you three *children* no longer play in the dirt." He dragged out the word "children," and a big grin covered his face. "Thought you'd outsmart me, didn't you?" He laid down his bike and sauntered in front of them, taking hold of Marc's bike in case he decided to whiz off while Mooney was on foot.

"Get out of my way, Mooney. I'd love to run you over." Marc caught hold of Bluedog, who had moved closer to him and started to growl. She got stiff all over and cocked her head.

"Why don't you sic that funny-looking dog on me?" Mooney dared. He moved over to Hermie and took hold of Hermie's arm. "I knew you boys had found something. You've been digging, haven't you? Slipped out in the night to try to outsmart old Mooney." He twisted Hermie's arm enough to make Hermie grimace. "Want to tell me about it, kid?"

Eddie dropped his bike. "You're a pile of horse pucky, Mooney. Pick on someone your own size." Eddie moved behind Mooney.

"You mean you, Greasehead?" Mooney started to laugh. He turned around to take care of Eddie. Eddie danced around him, fists up, like a terrier with a tiger.

"Take off," Eddie shouted, having maneuvered Mooney away from Marc and Hermie.

Marc motioned to Hermie, knowing that Eddie could take care of himself. What he lacked in size, he made up with nerve. And Marc figured Eddie could outrun Mooney if nothing else.

Sure enough, by the time Hermie and Marc pulled up quietly to Eddie's window, Eddie had caught up with them. He jumped off his bike, laid it next to the other two, then flipped open the window screen. "I always leave it open. Never know when you'll need to make a fast escape."

Marc smiled and shook his head. Eddie had his life under control, even if it wasn't perfect. They rolled into the low window as quietly as possible and lay on top of Eddie's bedspread. The bed shook with laughter.

"Shhh, they'll hear us," said Hermie, trying to hold back his giggling.

"No, they won't," said Eddie. "Remember? They can't hear."

"Mooney—Mooney—" Marc couldn't stop laughing to talk. "Did you see that look on his face when he saw us? It was almost worth getting caught."

"Yeah, he knew we'd outsmarted him." Eddie sat up. " 'Course that doesn't take much effort." He started laughing again.

Finally Marc rolled over. "Thank goodness we weren't carrying the relics."

"Yeah, Marc. That was good thinking." Hermie rolled onto his stomach.

"If I could sneak into the bathroom and clean up," Marc said, "I would go on home to sleep."

"Me too," Hermie said. "Except that I'm starving. I was looking forward to Gramma's biscuits and ham gravy."

Marc had forgotten that. He'd stay for sure if Gramma would cook for them. So they cleaned up as best they could without taking a bath, and appeared at Gramma's table for a suspiciously early breakfast before taking off for home.

Gramma, surprised but delighted to have three hungry boys to feed, made a big meal of hot biscuits, fried ham, and scrambled eggs, and gave them each a heaping plate. Without thinking, she even poured them coffee. Marc mixed his with thick cream and swigged it down, feeling warm to his toes.

When they were done, Marc felt doubly full. The secret of the cave filled and warmed him, too. They had made a special find. There were really no great relics in the grave, nor anything rare. The arrowheads were beautiful. But the fact that it was a boy who was close to their age buried there had made him possessive about the discovery. That was why he had insisted they not reveal the grave until he could think about it some more. Right now it belonged to them. If news got out, it would belong to the whole town. And the last person Marc wanted to share it with was Howard Moon. Even if they got credit for the discovery and the money from the reward, to share it with people like Mooney would spoil it.

At least he had bought some time from Hermie and Eddie. Now he had to decide what to do.

11

A TALK WITH MR. DANIELS

The first thing Marc did was get some sleep. Falling into bed the minute he got home, he stayed awake just long enough to feel Bluedog sneak into bed beside him. Mama never liked the idea of his sleeping with a dog, but now with her gone, they'd gotten into this new habit. He ran his hand across Bluedog's warm middle and was immediately asleep.

It was just past noon when he woke, hot and sweaty from sleeping in the daytime.

"You boys must have stayed up all night." His father came in from the office to get some iced tea while Marc was pouring himself a bowl of cornflakes. He wished he had some more of Gramma's good cooking.

"Yeah, sorta," Marc mumbled. He had hidden his dirty clothes under the bed. He smeared peanut butter on some soft white Wonder Bread, trying to keep it from tearing.

"I hope you didn't keep Mr. and Mrs. Sparks awake." His dad squeezed a slice of lemon into his tea and added three teaspoons of sugar.

"No, we didn't." Marc kept his answers short and pretended to be still half asleep. In fact, after he'd shaken off the heavy feeling from sleeping in the heat, he'd gotten so excited he could scarcely keep his secret. He wished he could tell his dad, but he wasn't sure how he'd react or what he'd say. He needed to share with someone—someone who would understand his feelings.

"Are we going to see Mama before Sunday?" he asked.

His father stood at the window, staring off into space. "Would you like to, boy?" he answered, finally.

Marc hated to admit he really wanted to visit Roy Clearwater just as much as he wanted to see his mother. But he'd give her a hug, talk for a minute. He figured it was his dad, not him, that she wanted to see anyway.

"Sure, why not? Let's go tomorrow. It's the middle of the week. If you aren't too busy . . ." Marc added, giving him a chance to back out.

"I'm never that busy. It's a deal."

When he'd finished eating, Marc took a glass of iced tea to the back step and sat there thinking. Bluedog brought her ball and looked up at Marc with a twinkle in her eyes. Did she know they shared a great secret?

"Isn't it too hot to play, Blue?" Marc took the ball. Bluedog waited, dying for Marc to throw it so she could bring it back. "Guess not." He tossed the ball to the back of the lot.

Weeds were getting high. Grasshoppers whirred and flew like popcorn popping when Bluedog chased the tennis ball to the corner of the fence. Maybe this evening he'd get out the scythe and cut the weeds. If Mama came home unexpectedly she would be disappointed in Marc and his father for letting the garden get into such a mess. But there was no chance of her coming home, so why bother? Marc didn't know why he even thought of it.

He heard Mooney's voice before he saw him coming toward the front of the house, Otis sauntering along beside him. What was Mooney doing at Marc's place? He didn't wait to see.

"Come on, Bluedog—come on, hurry!" Marc whispered to the dog, who held her ball for another throw. Grabbing his bike from the tree near the back door, he slipped it through the gate. Quietly he latched the gate shut. He and Bluedog were on their way down the street behind the house before Marc decided where to go.

He'd go talk to Mr. Daniels. He could talk to him in general without revealing their secret. It might help him decide what to do about their discovery.

"You must need something cold to drink, boy," Mr. Daniels said, when Marc came into the cool, dim store. He had three fans going. They stirred up a lot of dust, but at least they kept the air moving.

Marc didn't mind Mr. Daniels calling him boy. It was a habit lots of people in this town had, talking to kids. Marc knew Mr. Daniels wasn't thinking of him as a nobody. But his dad had been calling him boy for so many months now, Marc figured he'd forgotten his name.

Mr. Daniels sat on a stool behind a counter, fanning himself. His shirt was soaked clear through around the neck with perspiration.

"I sure could use something cold, Mr. Daniels. Now that it's stopped raining, summer has set in for real."

Mr. Daniels got two frosty RCs from the icebox in the back of the store. Marc pressed the cold bottle to his cheeks, then put his cooled hands to his neck. "Business slow?" Marc asked, to start a conversation.

"Pretty normal, I'd say. Relics are one of those things people can do without. Not many tourists coming here in the summer, either, on account of the heat. Can't say as I blame them. Fall and spring are better. I do a lot of my thinking this time of the year."

"I've been doing a lot of thinking myself." Marc eased into his subject.

"I've about forgot what a boy your age thinks on." Mr. Daniels leaned back on two legs of his stool. He had pulled up an old wooden chair for Marc.

"Oh, I think about being in the woods, swimming, exploring, finding something good. If we found something and told Mr. Beslow, I figure he'd want to go dig it up, don't you?" Marc sipped the RC, feeling tiny drops fizz onto his nose. He tried to act as if he didn't care about the answer—as if he were just asking.

"I reckon. He'd probably want to take it to the museum at the university and look it over. Decide how long it had been buried, what Indians left it there. You figuring on finding something?"

Marc took a big swallow of the RC. Bubbles exploded into his throat and nose. He choked, then coughed until he got control. Mr. Daniels was looking at him kind of funny when he came up for air. Or was it Marc's imagination?

"I figure I could," Marc said when he recovered. "It's possible, don't you think?"

"Anything's possible. Harder these days than when I was a boy. Sometimes I went down on the river bottoms and looked around. Picked up lots of spears and arrowheads that way. Awls and grinding stones. Graves were more often in some farmer's field.

"I wish I could have gone with you."

"Then you'd be old like me, Marc. And you couldn't go looking at all."

They both laughed, thinking about Marc being as old as Mr. Daniels. A peaceful quiet fell over them as Mr. Daniels teetered back and forth on his stool, and Marc listened to flies buzzing in the window behind him.

"How do you think the Indian people felt about your digging up their graves?" Marc asked finally. He badly needed an answer to that question.

"Don't reckon they cared much, seeing as how they'd been dead a long time. Don't figure they were standing around watching." Mr. Daniels laughed at the idea.

Marc had a hard time laughing with him. "Where do you figure they are now, those Indians?" he asked.

"Well now, that's a pretty big question, Marc. And I don't reckon anyone knows for sure. Some people believe we go sit on a cloud and play a harp. Or maybe sit in a big kettle with fire burning around us. I can't rightly say I believe that, and I never took much to playing a harp. Others think we sit out there someplace waiting to come back. At my age I'm not sure I want to go around thinking about it too much."

"Does it scare you, Mr. Daniels? Does dying scare you?"

"I'd be lying if I said it didn't, but everyone gets around to it in time. You know what they say—death and taxes . . ." Mr. Daniels took a sip of his RC. "Something we all get to do. What's got you into thinking about dying at your age, Marc? Your mama being sick? They don't think she's going to die, do they?"

"No. I guess she could, but she's getting better, I think. She has to stay in Boonville until she gets well. I was just thinking about it."

Mr. Daniels nodded as if he understood needing to think about things like dying. They sat silently again. One reason Marc liked coming to visit Mr. Daniels was that they could sit together, keeping each other company, without talking. Marc liked sitting there surrounded by all the junk in Mr. Daniels's store. Sometimes he wandered from table to table, counter to counter, looking and daydreaming.

It wasn't the uncomfortable feeling of quiet like there was at his house right now. Mr. Daniels and Marc didn't need to talk; Marc needed to talk to his father, but he didn't know how.

"I wish I could talk to my dad like I can to you, Mr. Daniels," Marc said finally. "He used to talk to me. We'd talk about relics and lots of things. Now he sits around all the time and acts like I'm not there."

"I reckon he misses your mama."

"I miss her, too, but why would that make him ignore me?"

"He's got something on his mind. Might be he feels guilty, feels it's his fault your mama got sick."

"How could that be true? How could it be his fault that Mama got sick?" That didn't make any sense to Marc.

"Of course it isn't, but maybe he thinks his bringing her down here from the city made her sick."

Marc couldn't think that Mama's moving to Pine Creek from Chicago had anything to do with her being sick. And, after all, it had been a long time ago, almost five years. What Mr. Daniels said didn't make any sense. But sometimes things adults said or did made no sense to him.

"I have to go home," he said abruptly. He was starving. Maybe he could talk his dad into eating in the cafe tonight. Then he'd get another decent meal. "Mr. Daniels, if Howard Moon should happen by and mention he's looking for me, would you tell him you saw me on my way to Fort Smith?"

Mr. Daniels smiled. "Having trouble with Mooney, huh? I can't say that I like that boy much. I don't reckon I'd want him for a friend."

"I don't even want him for an enemy." Marc thanked Mr. Daniels for the cold drink, called Bluedog from under a table near a fan, and took off down the highway for home.

When Marc called Hermie and Eddie, he found that

Mooney had paid them visits, too. "My mother told him I was asleep," said Hermie, who admitted he'd slept until three o'clock. "She thought I was sick. I pretended we'd sat up all night talking, the way girls do at sleep-over parties."

Marc laughed. Ever since the run-in with Louanne Swartzberger, Hermie had sworn off girls forever. He couldn't say anything good about them.

"Mooney came by while I was sitting on the porch with Pops," Eddie said. "Even old Mooney didn't dare threaten me with a grownup there. Pops had his hearing aid turned off, but Mooney didn't know it. Later Pops said he was glad I had a new friend."

Eddie and Marc laughed at that idea. Then they made up a plan to go into the cave on Thursday. Marc knew Eddie would wait if they had a definite plan to return. They also had to have a way to elude Mooney. Marc gave Hermie and Eddie that job.

Meanwhile, he kept worrying about his problem. Maybe it was wrong to disturb the Indian boy's grave.

12

ROY CLEARWATER

On Wednesday Marc and his dad left in time to get to the sanatorium by mid-morning. They'd have lunch with Mama and leave soon after, since she had to rest every afternoon.

Marc hugged Mama, who looked very pretty. She had left her hair loose, maybe hoping she'd get another surprise visit. "You two are spoiling me," she said.

"We like spoiling you, Mama," Marc said, handing her the few flowers he'd been able to save from the weeds in the backyard.

"Oh, my bachelor's buttons. I love this blue. They must look pretty in the garden. I'd love to see them."

Marc didn't say a word and was glad she couldn't see the mess their backyard had become. His mother looked frail and tired, now that he studied her up close.

"I had hoped I might be home by now to see them, but the doctor says I have to be patient. I'm afraid I'm not a very good patient." She laughed at the double meanings.

"Maybe this fall?" Marc's father came alive at the idea of Mama coming home.

"Maybe." Mama reached out and took her husband's hand. Marc looked at them and quietly sneaked away. They would never miss him.

He almost ran into a nurse outside Roy Clearwater's room. "Mr. Clearwater is having a good day, Marc," she said. The nurse was round and pink and smiled at him, making him feel super. He didn't realize she knew his name.

"Hello, Mr. Clearwater," Marc greeted him. "How are you?"

"I wish I could be outside." The old Indian was nearly always staring out the window when Marc came.

"I'll take you onto the sun porch," Marc offered. He went to get the nurse to help him get Mr. Clearwater into a wheelchair. He could walk around his room, but not all the way outside.

Mr. Clearwater grumbled, but went along with the work of getting him out onto the sun porch. Then he said, "This is fine, Marc, but I meant down in the woods, down by the river."

"Oh. Well, I guess you'll have to imagine being there. I can tell you what it looked like the other day, and you can pretend."

"I remember the long summer days," Mr. Clearwater said, not waiting for Marc to remind him, but beginning a story.

"I roamed the woods day after day. I hunted and fished for my family. Once when I was just a boy I carried a deer home. I could hardly manage the weight. My mother was proud."

"How did she make your food last through the winter?" Marc asked, although he thought he knew.

"She dried the deer meat and sometimes ground it with berries. She smoked the fish. Then we would have plenty if the winter was hard and we couldn't hunt."

"Did you have a gun or bow and arrows?" Marc asked,

remembering the single arrow in the grave they'd found. Also the perfect arrowheads, ten of them. He would like to bring both to Mr. Clearwater, who would probably be sure of the tribe.

"Oh, I had a gun. Not a very good gun, but I was proud of it."

Mr. Clearwater drifted back into those days, roaming the forests. Marc left him there for a few minutes. It was the only way he could enjoy the woods now. Then Marc asked another question.

"How did your people feel about dying, Mr. Clearwater? I know they buried things with the person who had died, things to keep him company on his journey, even food. How would they feel about someone digging up that grave now, studying your people?"

"Misfortune will happen to the best and wisest of men," Mr. Clearwater said, after thinking for a few minutes. "Death will come, and always out of season. A season of grief will come, then will pass away. I will not need my grave place in the spirit land. I will have my house, my tipi there, and I will be able to hunt the buffalo again."

Marc thought about what Mr. Clearwater meant when he said death would always come out of season. Maybe that a person was never ready for it? Or his kinfolk were never ready? Mr. Clearwater sounded ready. But even though Marc knew Mr. Clearwater might die soon, and Mr. Daniels might die before too long, he wasn't ready to let his two old friends go. Was that selfish? Would Mr. Clearwater be happier hunting his buffalo again? Would Mr. Daniels rather be digging on the river bottoms for Indian relics? Mr. Clearwater sounded sure of what he'd be doing in the spirit land.

Without meaning to, Marc saw his mother's face before him. The hollows in her cheeks. How tired she looked. She was young. It wouldn't be fair for her to die. It would be out of season.

He stared at the sanatorium grounds, plants and trees budding and leafing out, getting a good hold on summer—a good hold on life. It was summer, the best time to be alive.

He thought of the Indian boy from the grave, dying so young, certainly out of season. For a moment Marc could see him playing with his dog, shooting his bow and arrows, hunting rabbits. His constant thoughts of this boy, and his talks with Mr. Clearwater, had made Marc feel as if he had known someone whose childhood might have been like Mr. Clearwater's own.

Their discussion was interrupted by the bell summoning them to lunch. Marc turned the wheelchair around and pushed Mr. Clearwater into the hall and down to the dining room.

"Mama, you remember my friend, Roy Clearwater. He's a full-blooded Osage Indian." Marc reminded Mr. Clearwater that these were his parents, and they all sat together. They had met only one other time, since Mr. Clearwater usually ate in his room.

"Marc talks of you often, Mr. Clearwater," Mama said. "I've been meaning to come and visit. I've stayed by myself too much."

"Do you get lonely here, Mama?" Marc asked, not knowing if he wanted to hear her answer.

"Sometimes, Marc. But I remind myself I don't have to stay here forever, and that I have family who come to visit often." She smiled at Marc and his dad. "Family who love me." She reached over and patted Marc's hand.

"Marc is a fine boy," said Mr. Clearwater. "He would have made a good Osage."

Marc felt pride filling his chest, and he ducked his head, concentrating on eating. There was a good macaroni salad with tuna fish, and fruit salad with oranges, grapes, and shreds of coconut. His dad and Roy Clearwater talked about relics, and he listened, glad his father was interested.

"Good-bye, Mr. Clearwater," Marc said after lunch. Marc's father had said he'd push Mr. Clearwater back to his room for his rest. "I'll visit you on Sunday."

"Think of me when you're sitting by the river," he said. "Soon I will be fishing there."

"I will," Marc promised.

"Marc," said Mama, when they had gone, "I'm worried about your father. He seems tired and tense. I know he's worrying about me, and that's not doing any good. Have you been doing any spelunking since I left?"

"Who—me?" Marc said, feeling terribly guilty.

"You and your father. He really liked those trips you took together."

"Oh . . . no, he says he doesn't have time to go."

"He always says that. Insist that he go with you."

"Okay," Marc said. But Mama didn't understand how hard it was for him to talk to his father lately.

"And, Marc . . ." She took Marc's chin in her hand and looked right into his eyes, as if she saw a lot of stuff there Marc was trying to hide. "Be careful, will you? I need my family."

"I will, Mama." If she'd guessed Marc was keeping something secret, she didn't pry. She was always like that, trusting Marc, not making him tell her all his thoughts or all the things he was doing. But that made him feel even more guilty. He might have told her about the cave and the Indian boy, if his dad hadn't come back.

"Mr. Clearwater sent this for you." Marc's dad handed him something. It was the picture, the one of Mr. Clearwater.

"Why?"

"He just said he wanted you to have it."

"Time for your nap, Alina." His dad said Mama's name like it was part of a poem.

They walked her back to her room, and saw to it that she got into bed. "Remember when you used to try to make me take a nap?" Marc asked, laughing.

"I sure do. You needed less sleep than anyone I'd ever known. I thought all babies slept a lot."

"I wasn't a baby then. I was four."

"And into everything. I remember one day I found you into your father's rock collection. You were sitting there, carefully taking out each rock and looking at it. I figured you couldn't hurt them, and they were too big to swallow."

They all laughed and the good feeling from the visit followed Marc and his father to the car. Bluedog jumped in beside Marc and licked his face, glad to be going home. Marc put Mr. Clearwater's photo on the dash where he could see it as they drove.

Then he watched the mountains and trees go by on the curvy road. About halfway to Pine Creek he blurted out his thoughts. "Even if Mama died, she'd be here watching us when we needed her, don't you think?"

"Your mother isn't going to die, boy!" His father's voice was sharp, his sudden anger filling the car.

Marc stiffened and felt Bluedog come alert under his arm. She looked at him as if to say, "*What's wrong?*" Marc realized his dad didn't even like him to suggest that Mama might die. Death was not a subject he had thought about much before she had gotten sick and they'd found the Indian boy in the grave. But any fears that were on his mind seemed to have been laid to rest by Mr. Clearwater's words: *I will be able to hunt the buffalo again.*

Mr. Clearwater looked forward to going on to another place where he would be free of being old. Mama wasn't old, but maybe she was tired of being sick. And Marc knew her well enough to be sure that if the time came for her, she'd be ready. She never seemed to complain about bad things,

things like being sick and having to leave her family. She accepted them and made the best of them.

"Is that why you're so quiet all the time, Dad?" Marc asked. "Are you afraid that Mama is going to die?"

"I told you, boy, she isn't going to die." His father didn't look at Marc when he said that. His knuckles were white on the steering wheel. It was as if he thought if he kept saying it over and over it wouldn't happen, but Marc could tell he was afraid.

"Do you think it's your fault that she's sick?" Marc asked, remembering Mr. Daniels's idea.

"What makes you say that? That's ridiculous." His dad kept staring straight ahead down the road.

"I know you're worried about something all the time." It seemed to Marc that his questions were making his dad even more angry and upset. Marc squeezed Bluedog. She turned and smiled at him, then licked his face.

His dad got quiet again, but it wasn't the good quiet they'd brought from Mama and Mr. Clearwater to the car. It was the kind of silence you can reach out and touch, almost taste. It pressed against Marc, making him feel as if he couldn't breathe. Marc turned to the open window, but the air that came in was heavy and moist, clogging his nostrils.

Finally his father spoke. "Maybe—maybe if we'd stayed in Chicago . . ."

"Mama loves Pine Creek, Dad. She says that over and over. She loves her garden. Planting so many blue flowers around the vegetables. 'My blue garden,' she'd say. And remember that time when she went with us to the river to hunt arrowheads? We had a picnic on the sandbar. Then we all went swimming, even though the water was shallow. I don't think she got sick because she came here to live."

His dad's hands got even more tense on the steering wheel,

then he wiped the sweat from his forehead with the back of one.

"Mama's *not* dead, Dad. We can talk about her. It's all right to miss her. I miss her."

"I miss her, too."

Marc's throat tightened up, and he looked out the window. He watched the pine trees going by, even though they got blurry for a time. When he finally looked back at his father, tears were streaming down his face. He hadn't bothered to wipe them off. Marc looked away quickly and hugged Bluedog even harder.

After dinner Marc's father brought his coffee out onto the back steps instead of turning on the television. It had cooled off a little, and the evening was perfect. Cicadas had started up, enjoying an early concert. From somewhere in the distance, a mockingbird sang.

Marc had a glass of iced tea. He sipped the cool drink, figuring that if his dad wanted to talk, he'd let him start a conversation. But soon he got tired of the quiet.

"Mama would be ashamed of us, letting the yard go like this, letting her blue garden get so full of weeds."

"She sure would," his father said.

Bluedog moved up on the step and squeezed in between them. Marc put his arm around her and hugged her close. She licked his cheek and smiled at him.

"But Bluedog likes it. She scared a rabbit this morning. I hope they aren't silly enough to make a nest in there."

"I wouldn't be surprised if they did." His dad reached out and scratched Bluedog's ears, and she licked him, too.

"I guess I'll pull some weeds out of the roses. No use just sitting here."

Marc moved from the step and walked into the backyard. What a mess. He hardly knew where to start. But once he attacked a few of the weeds, he found the soil was still fairly loose from the rain, and the work was easy. A rhythm took over his body, and his mind drifted. When he looked up he found his dad had gone inside, but it didn't seem to matter. It felt good to do something for Mama. In just a short time he could see his progress.

His mind moved to the cave and to what tomorrow's trip might bring. Darkness caught up with him while he was still pulling weeds. Then, suddenly, an idea came to him out of the darkening sky.

He'd thought of a way to outsmart Mooney!

He dashed into the house, taking the steps two at a time. After washing his hands, he dialed Hermie. "Mooney has to run his paper route early, Hermie, right? Well, we get up at the same time and leave while he's out delivering. We'll try to avoid him, but if he sees us, he can't follow with a big load of newspapers. If he does, maybe he'll lose his job, and I can still get it." Marc had forgotten to ask Mr. Daniels about a job.

Hermie laughed. "Why didn't I think of that? It's too easy. Except for getting up at five in the morning ourselves."

Marc knew he wasn't going to be able to sleep late anyway, knowing they were going back to the cave. Eddie loved the plan, too. They agreed to meet at Hermie's place at dawn.

Their gear was already in the cave, so Marc didn't even have to get things ready. He just had to go to sleep as early as possible. That would be the hardest task of all.

13

EXPLORING THE CAVE

Marc groaned when the alarm clock under his pillow jangled. He hadn't fallen asleep until very late, and for a minute he felt as if he would never move again. Then excitement grabbed him, churned through his stomach. He sat up, causing Bluedog to jump and give out a soft "woof."

"Shhh—quiet, girl!" he whispered.

He stuffed his pillow and some clothes into the bedding and hoped if his dad looked in he'd think Marc was still asleep. Chances were, he'd not bother checking.

Just as he stepped out the back door, Marc heard a noise. *Ker-plunk.* The sound echoed through the still morning. He recognized the noise just in time to jump back inside. Mooney must have been threatened with losing his job. He was delivering papers extra early.

Grabbing his bike, Marc pushed it to the end of the driveway and watched as Mooney tossed papers down the block and turned off onto Dogwood Avenue. He figured Mooney would go the whole length of Dogwood. Then, even if he turned back toward the square, they'd be gone.

Marc rode fast in the cool morning air and slid to a stop in Hermie's driveway. Bluedog romped happily alongside. Marc was pleased to find Eddie and Hermie there, sleepy but ready to go. "Come on, hurry!" he whispered, as if Mooney could hear him. "Mooney is over on Dogwood. We can get away easily."

"Unless he has Otis guarding," suggested Eddie.

"Otis would never get up this early." Hermie yawned. "I must be crazy myself."

They made their escape and finally slowed their pedaling to a more reasonable speed. Marc did watch for Otis, but Mooney probably never figured they'd take off this early. They had outsmarted him.

The woods were cool and green and dripped with morning dew. Each time the boys had approached the cave entrance, they'd taken a slightly different path, so as not to set down a trail that could be easily followed. It meant getting wet from the moisture dripping from every bush, but there was no way around that.

Lowering Bluedog and swinging into the hole themselves had become routine. Soon they were walking down the tunnel, scrambling into the overhead passageway, and tumbling into the big room. Their footsteps and scuffling noises echoed off the rock walls.

"Well, shall we carry the relics out or get Professor Beslow to come in here?" Eddie asked as they squatted around the grave. Everything was exactly as they'd left it.

Marc looked at the skull, grinning up at them in the light from their headlamps. "Why do you suppose he was buried here, almost hidden in the cave?"

"I suppose someone wanted to be sure his grave was undisturbed for as long as possible." Hermie stated the obvious.

"I still think he died in the cave," Eddie said. "It was easier to bury him here than carry him out."

"I wish you hadn't said that." Hermie hugged Bluedog, who sat beside him. She had not whined or balked today, just trotted into the side tunnel with them.

"There's hardly anything here that's worth a lot, except for the curiosity of the grave being underground," Marc pointed out. "I'd like to cover it up and leave it alone."

"You mean not tell anyone? Ever?" Hermie asked.

"Holy Cow, you're crazy!" Eddie stood up. "Give up fifty dollars? That makes no sense at all. I can't think of one reason not to report our find."

"Because people hid the grave to begin with." Marc couldn't think of any way to explain his feelings. He wasn't even sure of them himself, but they had to do with respect for the dead and the Indian traditions. And maybe he had to admit to some sentimental idea of this boy being about their age—of his being buried with his dog. Maybe it was silly. Maybe Marc was being foolish. He could surely use his share of the fifty dollars. Who couldn't?

"I'll bet we could even get Beslow to raise the money to sixty, so we could each have twenty dollars," Eddie said, thinking aloud. "It's that good a find."

Marc had formed a picture in his mind since they'd found the grave. He took the chance of explaining it to Eddie and Hermie. "Listen, guys. Somehow this boy died, right? He was around our age. Unless there's another way into the cave, someone had to carry him down a rope, the way we came in. They brought him in here, scraped out this shallow grave, then brought in the rocks and dirt to cover him up. Someone went to a lot of trouble to bury him here. Sure, for a reason we'll never know—but a reason, nevertheless."

"You've thought about this too much, Marc." Eddie held a knife blade, chipped from flint, in his hand. He turned it over and over. "You've let your imagination run away with you." Eddie's voice was softer, less angry. Hermie said nothing.

The three of them sat quietly for a minute, staring at the skeleton and all the contents of the grave. Their lights bounced eerily off the cave walls and the shadowy pocket underneath the bluffs. Eddie laid the knife blade back alongside the boy's shoulder. He shook out the contents of the pottery jar, something none of them had thought to do before.

Marc shined his light on the things in Eddie's hand. A dozen or so grains of dry corn, and a circlet of blue beads intricately woven onto a piece of leather, darkened and stiff, preserved by the lack of air in the pot. Maybe it was a talisman, a good-luck piece of some sort.

"I'll bet his mother made that," Hermie said quietly. "What do you suppose it was?"

"A necklace maybe, something to ward off evil, keep him safe on his journey." Marc liked holding the beaded leather. It fit perfectly in the palm of his hand. He wanted to pocket it for himself, but if he insisted they cover up the grave, that meant leaving everything there.

"She might have made it for him when he was a baby. My mother made . . ." Eddie paused. "He might have been wearing it for a long time." Eddie wet his fingers and polished the dust off the beads. Now they could see the clear beads and the black ones that made the blue design stand out.

"It's pretty, isn't it?" Hermie spoke again.

"Look guys, it's early yet." Eddie put the talisman back into the jar and stood up. "Let's explore the other tunnel before we go back to town and get Professor Beslow." Eddie's voice was matter-of-fact, just as if Marc had never suggested they keep the grave secret.

"That's a great idea," Marc said. "Who knows? There might be more in here. This might be a place where they buried all their dead."

"If that's the case, then the cave would be sacred to them." Hermie stood up. "A sacred burial ground."

Marc liked Eddie's idea of looking around. They could do some more thinking while they explored. It would give Eddie time to think about the Indian boy. And if they did find other graves, it would change the whole picture. They'd have to report such a major find to a museum or the university.

"Let's go," Marc said, standing. "You game, Hermie?"

"I guess so. I've lived through getting here."

They laughed, and Marc felt his stomach relax. It had been feeling like a stretched-out rubber band all morning.

"Let's go look in my tunnel," Eddie suggested, and led the way back into the large room.

When they'd walked several hundred feet, they came to the first intersection. Eddie said, "Left." No one disputed his choice. Hermie and Marc followed, Bluedog hugging close to Marc again.

The cave walls were damp, so at one time there had been water in the cave. But there were not many good formations. More often there were piles of huge rocks, as if the earth had shaken and shaken, tossing boulders everywhere. Eddie left the path and peeked behind every heap, but he found no openings.

"Are you guys keeping track of where we are?" asked Hermie. "Like you said you did to keep from getting lost? Here's some short stalactites. They're a good landmark. I haven't seen any like this." Hermie shined his light to the left when they stopped to rest a minute. They crouched by a shelf that had leaned over so far they'd have to stoop and waddle under it to go on.

"It takes millions of years for the long ones to form,"

Marc told Hermie. "Each drop of water coming from over-head takes some lime out of the rock. That bit of lime is deposited on the end until it gets longer and longer. This cave is really old, but I wonder if there wasn't an earthquake here at some time. I've never seen such a jumble of piled-up rocks."

"Could there be another one?" asked Hermie, looking around.

"When do you remember there being an earthquake in Arkansas?" Eddie was impatient with Marc's lesson on how stalactites form. He waddled ahead, and Marc decided he'd better follow. "I think we're walking downhill and slightly eastward," Eddie said. "I'll bet we're getting near the river. Maybe it carved out this cave when it was cutting a path through the mountains."

"Then there should be another opening," Marc said, "Where the cave started from the river side."

"How can you all know what direction we're going?" asked Hermie. "You're just guessing."

"I have a super sense of direction," bragged Eddie.

Marc didn't say any more. He *was* guessing.

They scooted under the low overhang for about thirty feet, then the passageway opened again to a chamber about the size of Marc's bedroom. A breeze strong enough to ruffle his hair blew through the room.

"There is another opening," Eddie said with excitement.

"How can you tell, standing in here?" Hermie had decided it was time to eat. "I didn't have any breakfast," he said, in case anyone was against stopping again. He had carried a huge paper sack until they got to where they'd left their packs overnight. Then he'd emptied the contents of the sack into his pack and slung it over his shoulders.

"The air's coming in with such a strong breeze," Marc

answered, looking at Hermie's food. His stomach growled at the sight.

"I forgot about bringing food," Eddie admitted, watching Hermie open a peanut butter and jelly sandwich and take a big bite of it. Grape jelly stuck to the side of his mouth.

Marc had swallowed a glass of milk and eaten an apple on his way over to Hermie's, but that seemed like days ago. "Me, too. Have any extra, Hermie? I thought I'd be too excited to eat, and I hadn't thought about doing more exploring or being in here all day." Marc had actually been too excited to think, let alone eat.

"What would you guys do without me?" Hermie grumbled. "You may be expert cavers, but as expedition planners, you flunk."

"I came out the window." Eddie wet his finger and tested the air. "Gramma was already in the kitchen. She'd have fainted to see me up so early."

Marc had another excuse. "I had my mind on escaping Mooney."

Hermie pulled out two more sandwiches. "Well, I planned on sharing. I have some bologna sandwiches, too, and fruit, and a bag of leftover popcorn from last night. My parents always make popcorn when they're watching television."

Marc laughed. "Any iced tea or root beer?"

"Too heavy. Where's your water bottle?"

"Still in here from Monday night." Marc uncapped the bottle and took a swig to wash down the peanut butter. It tasted stale, but wet enough to satisfy his thirst.

After their small feast, Marc felt better and got up to lead. "Come on. Let's find the other entrance."

For an hour they wandered, partly following the draft which mixed musty cave air with fresh outside breezes. They paid little attention to the passing of time, but Marc felt confident he was mapping the cave in his mind. There were so many turns and twists, though, that sometimes he found loose rocks and made tiny cairns, or formed arrows pointing the way they'd come.

"Remind me to push these rocks to the side when we come back," he said.

"How come?" asked Hermie, watching Marc form an arrow with pebbles.

"It messes up the natural look of the cave."

"I like the idea of arrows pointing us all the way home." Hermie patted Bluedog. "Don't you, Blue?"

Bluedog whined and looked at them as if to say, *"Aren't you guys tired of being in here yet?"*

"That was a definite yes," translated Hermie.

Several times they had to choose between two tunnels. Twice they crawled a few feet, but they always came out to a place where they could stand. Some of the tunnels got very narrow, but none were so tight as to be scary.

"Boy howdy, this is some cave," Marc said. "We could spend all summer in here."

"You can spend all summer in here," Hermie said, but so far he hadn't complained about any of the crawling.

Once, looking up, Marc spotted a small cluster of bats hanging upside down. He tugged at Hermie's arm and pointed.

"Wildlife," said Hermie, grinning. "Neat. Will they bother us?"

"Of course not. They're not vampire bats," laughed Eddie. "They're big brown bats."

"Are there little brown bats?" asked Hermie, looking up.

"Yeah, but they live farther north. Bats don't come very far into a cave. There must be a hole to the outside somewhere near here." Eddie started looking.

"They can come in through small openings, though," Marc reminded Eddie. "I think we'd better go back the way we came in. We might never find another entrance our size. And it's noon."

"I can't keep up with the time underground, not seeing the sun move," Hermie said. "I guess my stomach would remind me, though."

"I wouldn't want to rely on your stomach, Hermie." Marc smiled. "It would always be lunchtime."

"Yeah, it is right now. Let's eat the other sandwiches. Then I won't have to carry them any farther."

They agreed, and when Marc bit into the bologna and cheese sandwich, he was grateful to Hermie again. "Every expedition needs a member who's aware of his stomach, Hermie. You can be ours. You get three stars for stomach awareness."

"What time did you get up to fix all this food?" asked Eddie.

"I made it last night." Hermie peered into his sack again. "I couldn't sleep, so I got up to eat. While I was in the kitchen, I decided it was as good a time as any to prepare for today. Mom was watching television, so she wasn't in there asking questions about so much food."

"Thanks, Hermie," Marc said. "I'll never tease you again about how much you eat."

"Or about losing weight, when you get stuck in a narrow crawl." Eddie took the last bite of his sandwich and licked his fingers.

Bluedog wasn't worried about anyone saving scraps, because Hermie had even included a small steak bone for her to chew on. Her gnawing helped fill the silence.

"How far do you think it is to the entrance?" asked Hermie.

"Not that far in a straight line," Marc said, "but we didn't come in a straight line. It will take us almost the same amount of time to go back as it did to get here."

"You sure you know the way?" asked Hermie for the millionth time.

"We're sure, Hermie," Eddie said. "Jeez."

Marc led when they started again. Before long, though, they came to a dead end. It didn't look familiar at all. Marc felt a shiver creep slowly up his back. "We weren't here before."

"Maybe we crawled out of one of those tunnels along here someplace." Eddie shined his light along the cave floor as they retraced their steps. "Here it is." He flattened himself in the dirt and wiggled into a hole he'd found.

Hermie and Marc crouched down, ready to follow, but Eddie's feet never disappeared. He wiggled out, a funny look on his face. His hair was full of dust. "It stops. Let's look around some more. I thought you marked all the places we came out of," he said to Marc in an accusing voice.

"I did. You saw me." Marc stood up and looked along the base of the wall for another tunnel. Let's retrace our steps slowly. I know we crawled just before we found the bats."

"Here it is," said Hermie. Marc could hear the relief in his voice. Marc had gotten turned around before in a cave. He'd learned not to panic, but Hermie didn't have the same experience.

Eddie went first again, turned, and called back to them. "Come on. I think we're on the right track now."

Hermie wiggled through, followed by Bluedog, who looked at Marc as if to say, *Do I have to do this?*

"Go on, Blue." Marc encouraged her and followed behind, pushing the dog when she stopped scrambling. Hermie pulled her from the other end. Eddie, still dubious about caving with a dog, went on without waiting for them to help her.

"Wait up, Eddie," Marc called, when he stood up. "Don't get too far ahead of us." Marc tried to shake off the funny feeling he'd gotten when they were back at the dead end, but he couldn't. More than anything, he wanted them to stick together.

"That tunnel seemed tighter than before," Hermie commented.

"That's because you ate two sandwiches," Marc teased.

"Well, I carried them all this way. I earned them."

Twice more they crawled in close succession, then the cave walls pinched down again. "We only went through crawl spaces this tight three times," Marc remembered. "And I'm not counting the slab we waddled under."

"This is going to sound silly." Hermie broke the silence that followed Marc's observation. "But I held my breath every time we crawled. I was that scared, but I hated to admit it. I had to stop and breathe halfway through the last two crawl spaces. They must have been longer—different ones."

"Why didn't you say so?" Eddie turned to Hermie angrily.

"I'm saying it now. I—I didn't think it was important. I might have forgotten. I might have breathed without knowing it. It's silly. Don't pay any attention to me. I just followed you two. We—we aren't lost, are we?"

"Of course not, Hermie," Marc reassured Hermie—and himself. "It's easy to get turned around in the dark. We must have come through a tunnel we didn't see earlier. All we have to do now is go back." Marc made it sound easy. He didn't want Hermie to be as worried as he was getting.

They went back. But they couldn't find any other trail except those they had taken to reach yet another crawl. Marc left Eddie, Hermie, and Bluedog sitting or leaning on the cave wall when they reached a spot that looked familiar to them.

"You stay here. I'll look around." Marc flashed his light in all directions and followed up a passageway where he had to turn and slide sideways to get through.

He might not feel good about what was happening to them, but no way was he giving up. He knew Hermie, and even Eddie, were depending on him. He did have the most cave experience. But it came to him as he walked slowly and looked in all directions, searching for something—anything—that looked familiar, that he didn't have the same feeling about this cave as he had about others he had explored with his father. Was it because his dad wasn't here? Was it the strange, massive formations? The lack of delicate soda straws and beautiful calcite flowers he'd seen in other caves? This cave seemed to be more of a home for gnomes and witches. Every cave had its own distinct personality, and this one was definitely spooky.

"Boy howdy!" he whispered. Eddie was right. His imagination was running away from him about ninety miles per hour. Not a good sign, thinking about weird stuff that could be in there with them.

He opened his eyes wider. They felt dry and gritty. He sniffed the air. It was mustier here. The draft had stopped. He tried to remember when he had first become aware of the breeze swirling around them. Then his light spotted another crawl space. Here was the one they'd come through to get off track.

He hurried back. "This way, Eddie, Hermie. I've found it." He heard the relief in his own voice now. It was definitely time to get out into the sunshine.

They practically ran back to where Marc had been exploring. There was a narrow slide-through to get there. Marc watched as Hermie barely pushed through, belly touching the wall on one side, rear end scraping against the other.

Eddie had slid through first. They caught up just in time to see him disappear into a hole near the floor. Marc knelt down to follow, but Eddie wiggled back out. "Dead end. It plugs up."

Marc had been so sure he was right this time. He'd ignored the fact that they hadn't come through the narrow spot, that there was no pile of rocks by the tunnel. Now his confidence was really shaken, but he turned around and started back without saying a word. He couldn't panic. Rule one: Carry enough light. Rule two: Don't let yourself panic. Marc wrote rule three at that moment: Don't think about how much time you've spent since lunch taking wrong directions; don't think about the fact that it's almost three o'clock.

"Let's backtrack all the way to where we ate lunch," Marc suggested when Hermie and Eddie caught up with him.

"Do you know how long we've spent messing around here?" Eddie said, breaking Marc's new rule three.

Usually Marc never worried about time. It didn't seem to matter. But if it took them five hours to get to their lunch spot, it would take them five hours to get back to the entrance—after they found the way. That would get them home at nine o'clock tonight. Even Marc's dad, even Pops and Gramma couldn't help but notice that. And Hermie would be conspicuously absent from supper.

"Do you have a better suggestion?" Marc put Eddie on the spot. If he was dying to take the lead, Marc would pass it over willingly.

"No." Eddie's face in the dim light of their carbide lamps was serious. His hair stuck out in all directions where the Brylcream held it stiff and greasy. It was full of cave dust. Suddenly Marc had this vision of him as an old man. But he didn't think Eddie would appreciate his mentioning that right then.

"How will we know when we find the lunch spot?" Hermie's voice wavered.

"I left my candy wrapper there," Eddie admitted.

Marc always picked up his trash. He'd noticed that Eddie usually did, too. For once Marc was glad he'd been careless.

"Bluedog probably left her bone," said Hermie. "Find your bone, Bluedog, find your bone."

Bluedog cocked her head and gave Hermie a puzzled look. They tried to laugh.

They couldn't find the candy wrapper. Or the bone. Once they stopped and refilled the lamps with carbide so they wouldn't go out. No one said a word as they performed the simple chore. After another hour, they had to admit they were in trouble. Marc didn't see how he could possibly have gotten this turned around.

The cave was the kind spelunkers call a maze. It twisted and turned and doubled back on itself time after time. But they'd always taken the obvious tunnel, the biggest one. And even mazes usually doubled back until they came to the main trails again.

The one thing keeping Marc from complete panic was that the draft started to blow steadily again, fresh and cool. But, taking a deep breath, he knew he had to face facts.

"I guess we're lost, guys," he said aloud, facing the truth himself and making Eddie and Hermie face it with him.

"Lost?" Hermie repeated.

The word echoed around them, bouncing off the cold, bumpy walls. Lost . . . lost . . . lost . . .

14

THE BEADED MOCCASIN

"Lost?" Hermie slid down the cave wall and crumpled into a heap as he said the word again. "I don't want to be lost in here." Maybe Bluedog heard the way Hermie's voice quivered. She came over and licked his hand.

"Shut up, Hermie," Eddie said. "No one *wants* to be lost. This isn't that big a cave, Marc. How can we be lost?"

"Maybe it's not big, but it winds around a lot. We must have taken some turn we never saw earlier. It threw us totally off track."

"This is your fault, Marc. You said you could keep the directions in your head, so I stopped drawing the map." Eddie's voice revealed his fear, but he turned it into anger, instead, and blamed Marc.

Marc did feel responsible for Hermie and Eddie, but he didn't like Eddie's saying it was his fault they were lost. Eddie had done almost as much spelunking with Pops as Marc had with his dad.

"Look, you know this can happen, Eddie," Marc leveled with him. "We can't panic. We have to sit down for a minute and decide on a plan. It may take us longer than we'd like, but we will get out of here."

"Want some popcorn while we think?" Hermie tried to be helpful in the only way he could.

"Maybe we should ration what food and water we have left," Marc said, and was immediately starving. He pushed away the thought of eating, digging in his pack for a stick of gum.

"We're not going to be in here for days, are we?" Hermie sounded panicky again.

"Of course not," Marc told him, and wished he believed it himself. "But if we could find a spot that looked familiar, I'd feel better."

"This is a bunch of horse pucky. Sitting here isn't doing us any good." Eddie got up and started forward. Marc knew they had to stay together. He pulled Hermie to his feet and followed Eddie. He liked Eddie searching better than Eddie sulking.

Looking carefully at every wall as they walked, they wandered in the cave. Bluedog was sticking tight to Marc's leg again. She whimpered. When he heard that, Marc had to fight down pure gut-fear that grasped and twisted his stomach.

He got colder and colder, but the palms of his hands started to sweat. He rubbed them on his jeans and pounded both arms to get them warm.

"I'm cold," said Hermie.

"Me too," Marc told him. "Rub your arms and keep moving."

Eddie had gotten ahead of them. Now he returned. Marc didn't like what he saw on Eddie's face. "This tunnel stops up ahead. There's no way out. I looked everywhere."

"It can't stop! We got in here somehow!" Marc shouted without meaning to.

"Well it does! Go see for yourself, Marc, if you don't believe me." Eddie crumpled down and buried his face on his knees.

Marc believed Eddie, but he had to look. He took off the way Eddie had come. Sure enough, the tunnel came to an abrupt end with a breakdown. Marc shined his headlamp up and down the walls, and into every crevice.

There was no crawl, nothing that even hinted of a way out. The walls were damp, and a tiny drop of water slid down to a slimy puddle on the floor. There was no air moving in the dead end, and there was a heavy, musty cave smell. Marc started to shiver like crazy. Icy fingers clutched the back of his neck. His teeth started to chatter. He took a deep breath and clinched his teeth tight. He couldn't go back to Hermie and Eddie until he got hold of himself. Not to mention Bluedog. He'd even gotten his dog stuck in this crazy mess.

"Anything?" Hermie asked hopefully, when Marc returned.

"No, it's obviously a dead end. We'll have to go back the way we came." Walking was better than sitting down and giving up.

"That's a dead end, too," Eddie said. "We're never going to find a way out. And it's all your fault, Marc!"

Eddie jumped to his feet and started swinging at Marc, fists flying. Marc jumped back, trying to catch hold of Eddie's arms. "Stop it, Eddie, stop it!"

Hermie tried to pull Eddie off Marc by grabbing him from behind. To their surprise, Eddie twisted away, fell to the cave floor and started to cry. Neither Hermie nor Marc knew what to do, so they let Eddie blubber until there was only sniffing left.

"Look," Marc said, finally. "We're all frustrated. We're

cold and tired, but we got in here somehow. So there's some way out."

Marc forced his voice to be calm, logical. But in his mind the whole cave had turned into a jumble of crawls, tunnels, piled rocks, winding corridors and places they'd squeezed through. Any mental map he might have had earlier was totally scrambled.

He sat down and tried to think. He wished he could cry, too. But he knew that wouldn't help. Hermie and Eddie were depending on him. What would be the best thing to do? They needed to raise their spirits. "Maybe it's time to eat the popcorn, Hermie. I'll take the chance on being hungry later."

Hermie was delighted to produce a wrinkled paper bag of semi-stale popcorn. As they dug in, no one complained that it was chewy instead of crisp.

Every few bites Hermie would toss a kernel into the air, and Bluedog would snap it into her mouth. She had always liked popcorn.

"Well, at least we've stopped feeding the hodags," Marc said.

"What—what are hodags?" Hermie stuttered.

"Holy Cow, Marc! Did you have to bring up hodags?" Eddie was angry again, but anger was better than crying. Marc had never seen Eddie cry, and it shook him almost more than being lost.

Marc laughed a little, wishing he hadn't thought of it himself.

"Hodags are cave creatures, Hermie. They're big and black and furry. They can hide easily, though, since all they have to do is slip behind a rock or down into a hole when we walk by. You can't see them in the shadows, either."

"This is some kind of joke, isn't it, Marc?" Hermie stuffed a handful of popcorn into his mouth, as if the food would protect him.

Eddie forgot his anger and his crying. Teasing Hermie was a way to forget their problem. "No one knows, but everyone who does any caving believes in hodags. You know what they eat—huh, do ya, Hermie, do ya?" Eddie hovered over Hermie, twisting his face into a distorted shape, holding his flashlight under his chin to make it worse.

"I don't want to know, you guys!" Hermie was near tears, and they should've stopped, but Marc couldn't.

"They feed on fear, Hermie," Marc whispered. "They've loved having you in here. They've probably eaten enough to last them weeks." Eddie and Marc laughed at the look on Hermie's face.

Eddie couldn't stop either. "They have only one eye, Hermie. It's in the middle of their foreheads, right here." Eddie poked his forehead. "You want to know how they mate, Hermie—huh, do ya, Hermie? They're eye-sexual. Get it, Hermie? Eye-sexual."

"Yeah," Marc added. "When they mate they do it by trading eyes. If you happen to be looking at them at just the right time, you'd know what they were doing. Cause you see a red flash when they do it."

"Yeah, they're speedy devils. Look, Marc, I thought I saw two doing it right now. Over there, look!"

Hermie covered up both ears and shut his eyes tight. "Cut it out, you guys."

All of a sudden, it stopped being fun to tease him. They got quiet. Too quiet. They remembered they were in a whole lot of trouble.

Eddie jumped up and went off into the darkness. Hermie sat whimpering, sounding as bad as Bluedog did sometimes. Marc felt awful, so he tried to empty his mind and not think of anything.

He didn't want to, but right away he thought of the dog's skeleton lying beside the Indian boy. Had the boy and the dog really died in the cave, and had his folks decided to bury him here? Maybe Bluedog wasn't the first spelunking dog ever. Maybe the Indian father and mother hadn't carried them in here for burial. Maybe they were already in, and they just didn't carry them out.

Maybe they'd put a curse on the cave—like in Egypt, in the mummy's tombs. Maybe if you disturbed this boy's grave something awful would happen to you. Like getting lost, and starving. First you'd go crazy, and then you'd starve.

Stop that kind of thinking! Marc ordered himself. They weren't going to die in this cave. But no one knew where they were. He could have at least left a note somewhere in his room—under his pillow, in a dresser drawer. *Stupid, Marc, really stupid.* Another caving rule: Tell someone where you're exploring.

His dad would eventually search to see if there was a clue as to where the three of them had disappeared. He'd find the caving gear gone. But he'd hunt in all the obvious, well-known caves first. No one knew about this cave. It hadn't been discovered for maybe a hundred years. Only the Indians knew about it.

Lost for a hundred years underground? Every turn Marc's mind took led to something worse, something he shouldn't think about. He needed some positive thoughts badly. He thought about covering the grave and leaving it hidden. What a great secret that would be for him to keep as long as he lived. How long was he going to live? Another couple of days? How long could they survive in the cave without food or water?

Eddie came back and slid down against the wall again. He said nothing. What good was it doing for them to all sit there, getting more scared by the minute?

A scratching sound interrupted their thoughts.

"What's that?" Hermie looked all around in a panic. "There's someone in here with us!"

"Holy Cow, Hermie, don't be silly." But Eddie looked around, too. There was definitely a noise that none of them was making. Bluedog whined, and Marc clamped her muzzle shut.

"Sounds like a mouse," Hermie said.

They all laughed a little. The idea of someone being in there with them was too scary. Besides, who could be in the cave with them?

"There are no mice in caves, Hermie." Eddie started acting cocky again. "Maybe a cricket or a salamander, if there's a pond. But no mice. Maybe it's a bat."

"Bluedog wouldn't whine at a mouse or a bat," Marc said, hugging her.

"A bat doesn't scratch around. They're all asleep," Hermie said. "At least the ones I saw were asleep. Maybe it's night and we don't even know it. Maybe all the bats are leaving the cave to go eat insects. We've stayed in here till dark."

Marc didn't want to think about it being dark outside. He looked at his watch. It wasn't dark yet, but it would be getting there fast.

"Packrats sometimes build nests inside a cave," Marc said. "But near the entrance, not this deep inside."

"Unless we're close to the outside and don't even know it." Eddie jumped up and shined his light in the direction of the noise. It sounded again.

"It sounds as if it's right over our heads." Hermie shined his headlamp up close to the top of the cave wall, too.

A slab of rock hung out over them and was definitely not attached to the ceiling. But they couldn't see over it.

"I'll boost you up, Eddie," Marc said. "I've got a good feeling about that ledge."

"I can't believe there's anything up there. The rock is too close to the ceiling," Eddie protested.

"Look anyway," Marc insisted.

Marc cupped his hands into a step for Eddie. He swung his foot up, and as soon as he had his balance, Marc lifted him until he could grab the edge.

"Be sure it's solid before you put your weight on it." Marc didn't want any of them hurt. That would only complicate their situation.

"It is. And Marc . . ." Eddie stared into the darkness.

"Yeah? What do you see?" Marc's hopes rose.

"I think I can feel a draft up here." Eddie's voice sounded hopeful again, too. "But . . ."

"What is it?" *Please, please let this be a way out.*

"It's a narrow crack between the ceiling and this ledge. It looks like it's awfully tight, Hermie."

"If it goes outside, I'll make it. I'll flatten myself like a pancake. You're not going to leave me here, now that you've eaten all my food."

"Can Bluedog make it?" It was the first time Marc regretted bringing her.

"I don't know. She's skinny enough, but what if it's a long crawl?"

"I'll keep pushing her. I can't leave her here."

Marc would keep looking until he found another way out before he'd leave Bluedog. They could send Eddie for help if Hermie or Bluedog couldn't make it. There were all sorts of possibilities now. Marc wished he hadn't left the rope at the entrance, though. He could have tied it around Blue and pulled her through a long crawl if he had to.

"Should I go all the way through, first, to be sure it's not a dead end?" Eddie asked.

Eddie had definitely been shaken up. Usually he'd never ask Marc's permission to go on ahead. He got ready to enter the hole he'd found. Perched precariously on the ledge, he took off his pack to push it ahead of him in the narrow space.

Marc thought for a moment. He wished he could see the crack. "No, let's stick together. We can all back out if we have to, but I have a good feeling about this."

"I'm glad someone does." Hermie was getting cold feet. "What if I get stuck?"

"We'll push or pull until we get you out." Marc laughed. "I read about a guy who got stuck. He went into the hole easily, but they had to pull him out. Broke his collarbone when he finally popped out like a cork."

"Thanks a lot for that encouraging story." Hermie got ready for Marc to give him a boost.

"This is the worst part." Marc joked and groaned before he even tried to lift Hermie. "You have to lose some weight before we take you in a cave again, Hermie."

"Good. I'll get fatter and then I can stay home and read about you all getting lost."

"Aaaaaagh." Marc exaggerated, but his effort was real. Hermie was no lightweight to boost up, like Eddie was. If he fell back, he'd squash Marc flat. Eddie was also part fly. He could stick to a rock that seemed to have no knobs on it at all and climb on up. Marc's arms started to shake, and he thought Hermie would never get onto the ledge.

Finally, Marc felt him lift his weight, then watched him swing and struggle to get a leg up onto the rock. "Tell me if you're going to fall back, Hermie, so I can get out of the way."

How easy it was to tease and joke, now that it looked as if they'd found a way out. Marc took a deep breath and hoped again that the crawl went through. It had to. He didn't think any of them could handle another disappointment.

"Is there room for you to sit and help Bluedog onto the ledge?" he asked, when Hermie seemed to be secure.

"I'm not sure. If she gets excited, she'll knock me off."

"I'll tell her to be calm."

"I'll have to start her through the tunnel in front of me," Hermie said. "There's not room for all three of us up here."

"Okay, here she comes." Marc had found a small bump he thought he could stand on once he got Bluedog started up. He'd lean on the wall and boost her higher.

On the first try, they both slid back to the cave floor. Bluedog started to bark. "I told you not to get her excited," Hermie called down.

"Blue, calm." Marc held her head between his hands. "Calm, you have to be calm."

Bluedog wiggled all over. This was a fun game to her. But Marc wasn't sure he could get her onto the ledge. "Calm," he said, and boosted her again. Her toenails scratched on the cave wall.

"Stop wiggling, Blue." Hermie leaned down to grab hold of her.

Marc almost started laughing at the idea of a chain of boys and dog linked together. If he laughed, they'd fall again. He ducked his head and let Bluedog stand on his shoulders.

Finally Hermie tugged her onto the ledge. Then he almost lost his balance as she licked and licked his face.

"Careful," Marc called. "Just stick her into the hole."

"That's easier said than done." Hermie tried to stuff Bluedog into the crawl space. "Go, Bluedog, go in there. Squish down." Hermie giggled, pushing Bluedog and sliding behind her. "She doesn't want to go."

"Tough. Holler to Eddie to call her." Marc knew Eddie had gone on through instead of waiting for them like he was supposed to. One good thing—if Eddie hadn't come back by now, the crawl must go through. Or—or he was still in it. Marc prepared himself. No caver likes to crawl far, especially when he doesn't know how long the tunnel is and where he's going to come out.

In seconds, Marc had pulled himself up onto the ledge. He stopped thinking, pushed his pack ahead of him, and started into the tight crawl space. He had to flatten himself totally. If he raised his rear at all, it kept him from going forward.

Hermie was still wiggling in front of Marc. He had taken off his pack and tied it to his foot, dragging it behind so he could push Bluedog ahead. Marc pushed both his pack and Hermie's.

Please, please let this go someplace. It would be terrible for all of them to have to back out. Sides of the crack started to close in. Then Hermie stopped.

"What's the matter?" Marc asked. His voice sounded hollow in the tunnel. He tried to keep focused on the cold air blowing over them.

"I think I'm stuck."

"No, no, you aren't. Push. Are your arms flattened out in front of you?" Marc fought the feeling of being trapped in the hole behind Hermie. Too late, he realized they should have gone through the crawl one at a time, so there would always be two to help if one got into trouble.

The feeling of rock pushing against him from every direction started to get to him. Suddenly he had to fight the urge to stand up, to scream, to get out of the crawl. *Calm, Marc. Calm,* he told himself, just as he'd encouraged Bluedog. *Think of Hermie. Think how awful it would be to think you were stuck.* "Are you pushing?"

Hermie moved an inch. "I'm trying!"

"Don't panic, Hermie. Take a deep breath, and when you breathe out all the air, push forward. Move a little at a time. Push hard."

Hermie did as Marc said and started to inch forward a little. Marc laid his head on his hands and rested. *Don't think about where you are. Don't think about the rock walls closing in on you.*

"I'm coming out." Hermie's voice was relieved and excited. "I'm coming out!"

Bluedog barked. Eddie had gone back into the crawl space and pulled her forward. When Hermie had stopped thinking about the dog and worried just about himself, he'd managed to pop out of the tight place and slide out onto the breakdown of dirt and rubble beside Eddie and Bluedog. Marc inched through the narrowest part of the crawl, then scooted quickly forward and out.

"Jumpin' Jehoshaphat," he said, belly flopping onto the pile of dirt and sliding down to sit beside the rest of the cave expedition. "I thought I'd be in there forever. I hate doing long crawls like that."

"You thought *you'd* be in there forever? What about me?" Hermie sat, hugging Bluedog. His face was the dirtiest Marc had ever seen it. And the happiest.

Shining his light on Eddie, Marc realized something was wrong. "What's up, Eddie? We're out of there. The crawl went someplace." They were in a small room, the best Marc could see. The air smelled really fresh, as if they were close to the outside.

"I—I—There was someone in the tunnel ahead of me."

Both Hermie and Marc were speechless. Finally Marc said, "That's impossible."

"No. I—I saw his foot."

"You saw his foot?" Hermie asked. "What did it look like? You're trying to scare me again, aren't you? You planned this for a joke because this is my first time in a cave. A sort of an initiation. I'll bet we weren't even lost. You said that we were and told me all that stuff about hodags, to scare me."

"Believe me, Hermie," Eddie was starting to talk normally. "We were lost. We may still be lost. And I'll swear I saw something in the tunnel ahead of me."

"What did the foot look like?" Marc asked again. "Did it have a shoe?" Marc half thought Eddie was joking, too, but he looked pretty odd.

"It—it—" Eddie started to stutter again. "It was wearing a moccasin."

"Oh, sure." Marc knew Eddie was teasing them now. "Boy howdy, we'd better get you out of here, Eddie. You're losing it."

Eddie jumped up and shouted. "I'm not kidding, Marc. There was a foot ahead of me in the crawl and it had on a moccasin. The moccasin had blue beads on it. It was brown suede and had designs in blue beads. You don't have to believe me, but I saw it. I know I did!"

15

TWO SECRETS

Put so strongly, Marc had to believe Eddie thought he saw something. But he couldn't believe it himself. They had all talked so much about the Indian boy and the grave that it was perfectly possible Eddie, scared and tired, could have imagined something in the darkness.

Maybe he'd seen the packrat that had made the scratching noise above them. They were obviously close to the outside. The packrat had come snooping around. Lucky for them, he'd come out on the ledge. Then he went back down the tunnel. Eddie had caught up to him, and just for a minute the packrat had looked like a brown moccasin.

"Okay, okay, you saw a foot." Marc decided to humor Eddie. "Let's look around. I think we're almost out of the cave."

"You don't believe me, do you?" Eddie gripped Marc's arm.

"It doesn't matter if I do or I don't." Marc shook Eddie's

hand off and started forward. "What matters is that we get out of here."

Eddie's face took on a sullen look, and he waited until Hermie and Bluedog followed Marc. He brought up the rear. Marc didn't care how Eddie felt. All he could think of was seeing daylight.

The room was about ten feet across, then made a turn to the right. On each side of a corridor where they could stand upright, there were hollowed-out ledges and pillars. The posts were smooth and the ledges were shallow. There were circular marks in the rock as if water had swirled inside the cave for centuries, carving them out. It confirmed Marc's idea that the river had cut out this cave as it eroded its way into the valley.

Rounding a corner, Bluedog stopped and started to whine. They all three stopped behind her and peered into the dim light that their lamps threw onto the cave walls ahead. They could barely see that the path started uphill and split off into two directions. Another decision. Marc was sick of making decisions. He wanted out of the cave. He'd had enough caving, enough adventure for one day—maybe for the whole summer.

"What's wrong with your dog, Marc?" Eddie was still angry.

Marc knelt beside Bluedog and patted her. "I don't know. This is the way she acted before I found the grave."

"Maybe she wants to get out of here," said Hermie. "I know I do. But she's making me nervous." Hermie knelt on the other side of the dog. "What do you see, Blue? Do you hear something? Dogs can hear better than we can."

"Holy Cow, Hermie. Everybody knows that. You think we're dumb?"

"What's the *matter* with you, Eddie?" Hermie said, tired

enough to stand up to Eddie. "Stop trying to pick a fight and help us decide how to get out of here."

Before anyone could decide, Marc looked up. In the dim light their lamps threw across the room, someone appeared in front of the tunnel on the left.

It was a boy just about their age. He was naked except for a loincloth. His skin was dark, his hair jet black and straight to his shoulders. A small piece of rawhide circled his head, holding his hair in place. On his feet were the brown moccasins that Eddie had described. Sure enough, they were beaded in turquoise blue. And around his neck, hanging on another piece of leather string, was the blue medallion they had found in the grave.

Marc blinked—once, twice. Was he dreaming? Hallucinating? He squeezed his eyes shut, then looked again and the figure disappeared into the tunnel on the left.

"Did you see that?" Marc whispered.

"What?" asked Hermie. "Are you all right, Marc? Stop standing there. We want to get out of here."

"You didn't see anything up ahead of us?" Marc had thought Eddie was seeing things because he was tired. Now he was doing the same thing.

Eddie stared at Marc. "Look, we're all tired. I'm getting out of here." Eddie headed for the right-hand passageway.

"This way, Eddie," Marc said, starting to the left. "This is the way out."

"What makes you so sure?" Eddie asked. "I say we go this way. You have a map?"

"I—I—"

They stood there in the black, cold silence, broken only by their breathing and the beams from three faltering flashlights and three dim headlamps. Marc's light went out. He beat on the end with the bulb.

"I'm leaving," Eddie said. "You coming, Hermie?"

Hermie looked at Marc. "What did you see, Marc?"

Eddie stared at Marc again.

"Nothing—it was nothing. Come on, I have a strong feeling that we should go to the left." Marc started in that direction and Hermie followed. Eddie had no choice but to come along.

Bluedog trotted just ahead of Marc, as if nothing had happened. There was no more whining, barking, reluctance to go forward.

"Bluedog likes this way," Hermie pointed out.

The space pinched down some and was filled with smooth stones like those in a creek bed. Their shoes crunched and rattled against the rocks. No one said anything. They kept going forward, following Bluedog, crawling after a short distance, even though the stones bruised their knees and hands. The tunnel was just Bluedog's size.

"Light! There's light up ahead!" said Eddie. He moved faster, past Marc, even though he was bent double, waddling like a duck. Marc was still crawling, too tall to squat for long.

Never had sunshine looked so good. They burst out of the cave onto a ledge and belly flopped to look around. Far below, the river meandered along. They were high up on the bluffs.

"Boy howdy, this looks good," Marc said. "I thought we'd be in that cave forever."

"*You* did." Hermie rubbed his eyes. "I thought we were going to die in there. That Indian boy died in there. I know he did. He got lost and—" Hermie started to ramble, as if he couldn't stop talking once fresh air had filled his lungs.

Marc and Eddie burst out laughing at the same time. Marc put out his hand and Eddie slapped it. Bluedog whined and licked Marc's face.

"How will we get Bluedog down from here?" Hermie asked.

"I should have brought the rope," said Marc.

"The strap on the bottom of my pack comes off." Hermie sat down and began to unfasten it. "It's not that long, but it's wide."

"We can add my belt to it." Marc unbuckled his leather belt. It was the first time he'd thought about using it.

Quickly he looped it around Bluedog's middle. Then Hermie slipped his backpack strap under the belt, knotting it on top. They tied the rope into a loop they could hold.

"You're a doggie suitcase, Bluedog," said Hermie, patting her on the head. Bluedog no longer protested any of the strange things the boys did.

It took an hour to work their way down the slope. Much of the rock was rotten and not good for climbing. Time after time they slid, starting tiny avalanches of rock and dirt. Sometimes they had to lower Bluedog on the strap. But there was no more fighting or arguing. They all helped each other and Bluedog. As they dropped lower, the bushes and undergrowth got thicker. They plowed through it, making a path. They ignored the scrapes and scratches of the branches; they were happy just to be outside.

"We're going to get covered with ticks," said Hermie.

"Who cares?" answered Eddie.

There was a drop-off if they went straight to the river, so they cut back toward the direction of the highway. As soon as they got lower, Bluedog, freed from her harness, bounced and ran to lap up the muddy brown water.

The boys followed her and, late as it was, they took time to shed shoes and socks and wade in the warm water. Sitting there on the bank, watching Bluedog snap at bees, they fell deep into their own thoughts. Marc's were mostly about being thankful they'd gotten out of the cave—and about the help he knew they'd had. It was not his imagination. He knew he had seen the—the Indian boy.

Hermie finally broke the silence. "I was afraid it'd be dark when we got out. We weren't in there as long as I thought. It's only six o'clock."

"If we'd gone back the way we came in, it would be the middle of the night. Getting out seemed longer, too, since we were turned around." Marc refused to say lost again. He didn't want to think about it. "But we were in there about ten hours."

Another silence. "What was it you saw, Marc?" Eddie asked.

Now, out in the lingering light of day, Marc thought about his experience. A part of him was sure he had seen the boy. But maybe he'd been thinking about him so much all day that he'd imagined it. Bluedog did act funny. Eddie did think he saw something earlier. But neither Eddie nor Hermie saw what Marc saw—thought he saw.

"Why were you so sure about which way to go, Marc?" Hermie joined the questioning.

"It felt right. And Bluedog seemed to want to go that way." Marc hugged her. He'd give her the credit. At least until he thought all this over again. Maybe some day he'd tell Hermie and Eddie what he'd seen. But right now it was much easier to say Bluedog had decided than to believe he'd seen a—a ghost. It was even hard to say the word. He'd never believed in ghosts, in spirits who hung around after bodies were dead. But now . . .

"It was a miracle we found our way out of there," Hermie suggested. "I don't ever want to go into a cave again."

"Yeah, a miracle." Eddie had been awfully quiet all the way down the mountain. "Marc—" he paused, looking Marc straight in the eyes, as if he was still thinking about being in the cave. "I—I think we should cover up the grave and leave the things there." Eddie made the suggestion as though it were a brand-new idea. As though Marc hadn't thought of it earlier. As though they'd never argued about it.

Hermie agreed. "Yeah, let's not tell anyone we found him."

Marc wondered if Hermie realized he'd said "found *him.*"

"We could push that big rock over the hole." Eddie went on.

"How about the hole on this side?" Eddie looked back the way they'd come, down the bluff. They had walked too far to see the ledge overlooking the river.

"I looked back up there after we got down," said Eddie. "You can't see it because of the way the ledge tilts up. You'd have to climb right up there before you'd see it. I hardly see anyone on the river way down there. Everyone climbs up by the swimming hole where the rock is solid."

Eddie scratched in the mud with a stick. "If it stayed hidden this long, it should stay hidden for a lot more years."

Marc didn't feel he had to agree, since he had made the suggestion in the first place. He didn't even care if Eddie thought it was his idea. All that mattered to him was that they leave the relics, the skeleton, there. Maybe, just maybe, each of them could take one of the creamy white arrowheads to remember him—the boy—by. As if they could forget.

"We can come back in a few days—let Mooney's curiosity cool off. Then we can outsmart him one more time." Marc stood up. "I may be in trouble for a few days anyway." *If anyone noticed I was gone,* he added to himself.

"Me, too. I've already missed supper." Hermie swung his pack on, light now without the food.

No one spoke until they got to town and were ready to head toward their own houses.

"Maybe we can go back on Saturday, even Sunday," Marc said. "Lots of newspapers to fold on Sunday." He waved to

Eddie and Hermie, and called Bluedog to follow him. She looked tired, but she smiled up at Marc and trotted along in a slow rhythm.

To Marc's surprise, his dad was in the backyard, digging at weeds with a hoe. He looked at Marc, but didn't stop him from going into the house. Marc came back out with a glass of milk and the hot dog that was waiting on his plate at the table.

He perched on the step and watched his father while he ate. He had given Bluedog a dish of dog food and a bowl of water, but she watched him eat first, hoping for some leftovers.

His dad leaned the hoe on the little shed that held all the garden tools—and the climbing ropes, Marc realized. And his own spelunking gear. Without saying anything, Marc's dad went inside, then came back out with a Coke. He sat beside Marc.

"Good cave trip?"

A bite of bread stuck in Marc's throat. "How'd you know?"

"Pillows in the bed made me think you'd left pretty early and didn't want anyone to know you were gone. Looking in your closet and the shed told the rest of the story." His dad tilted the Coke bottle and said no more.

"We were lost for a time," Marc confessed.

"Scare you?"

"Some."

"Learn anything from it?"

"A lot."

Cicadas sang about the sunset being over. A mosquito buzzed by Marc's ear. He waved it away. In the distance a mixed-up rooster crowed. Marc waited to see what his father would say next. To find out how much trouble he was in. Being in trouble was almost welcome. Maybe it would mean his dad cared that Marc had gone off and almost not come back.

"Your mother called me tonight."

"Is she all right?" Marc hated to think Mama had gotten worse while he was off fooling around.

"She says the doctor thinks she might be able to come home this fall. She's much better, and if she can get her strength back—well, it's a possibility."

"That's great." Marc felt relieved and gulped down the rest of his hot dog. Nothing had ever tasted so good. And now Mama was better.

"And, Marc . . ." His father had sat quietly while Marc ate.

"Yeah?" Marc patted Bluedog on the head. There was no sandwich left for her.

"Your mother asked me to tell you that Roy Clearwater died. She figured you'd want to know."

For a minute Marc sat stunned. He had known this could happen any time, but . . . Then across his mind floated a picture of the old Indian, sitting on the side of a river, fishing. Another picture followed. He was hunting for a deer, and he had a smile on his face.

"Marc," his father asked, "Are you okay?"

"Yeah, Dad, I'm okay." And he was. Marc knew that Mr. Clearwater was happy now. He wasn't cooped up in the sanatorium, waiting, wishing . . .

"I've been thinking we'd better not let your mother see her garden so full of weeds," his father said, reminding Marc that Mama was alive and coming home before too long.

Bluedog came up and put her nose on his dad's knee. She looked up at him with a smile he couldn't resist. He put out his hand and rubbed her ears.

"Would you help me dig, Marc?"

"Sure, Dad. And maybe—maybe if we get finished by this

weekend . . . well, would you like to see the cave we discovered? It was hidden, so hidden that maybe no one has been in there since Indians lived here."

It took his dad such a long time to answer, Marc didn't know what to think. He almost wished he hadn't asked, hadn't revealed the secret.

"I—I'd like that, Marc. I feel like you've been gone longer than all day. Or—or maybe I've been gone."

All the fatigue from the exhausting cave trip fell away from Marc's shoulders. He sat up straighter. Bluedog, sensing the change, ran to get her tennis ball. She wasn't tired anymore, either. She held the ball so either of them could throw it. They laughed at her, she looked so eager.

"Did Bluedog go into the cave with you?"

"Yes, it was quite an adventure, spelunking with a dog."

"I'll bet."

"Dad. There's one thing you have to promise me."

"What's that, Marc? I'll try."

"Can you keep a secret? You have to promise me you can keep a secret, before I can show you this cave."

His dad took another swallow of his cold drink. "I think I can, Marc. I've been known to keep a secret before."

"That's great." Marc got up and went to take a turn with the hoe. He realized that his arms were sore from hanging onto Bluedog all the way down the slope, boosting her and climbing in the cave. But he didn't care. Working in the yard felt good.

Everything was going to be okay. He knew it was. And deep inside he carried a warm secret.

Two secrets: the cave and the Indian boy. Two secrets that would be with him all the rest of his life.

AUTHOR'S NOTE

This story takes place in 1954. At that time collectors like Marc, Hermie, and Eddie, as well as Mr. Daniels, were not so aware that Native American artifacts are a valuable part of our culture, the history of our country. They enjoyed them for what they were, but felt that whoever found them had a right to keep them. They grew up hunting for arrowheads, Indian pots, and other relics near their homes.

In the 1920s and 1930s, when Mr. Daniels collected, most people didn't even want the artifacts they found. They didn't think they had any value at all. Dealers and collectors probably saved many of the relics that have found their way into museums today.

If you should have the good luck to discover an ancient site or other buried treasure from the past, such as dinosaur bones, do not dig or try to excavate in the area by yourself. Call an archaeologist, perhaps at a local college or university, or someone in the National Park Service.

You will receive credit for the discovery, but trained professionals should make the excavation. They can tell a great deal about the past lives of people in your area while they work. You may be able to participate in the dig under the supervision of these professionals.

By sharing your good fortune, all the world can enjoy your contribution to history. It is as important for us to preserve the relics of our past as it is for us to preserve the unique character of our lands.